TEAM
FUGEE

TEAM FUGEE

Dirk McLean

James Lorimer & Company Ltd., Publishers
Toronto

James Lorimer & Company Ltd., Publishers acknowledges the support of the Ontario Arts Council (OAC), an agency of the Government of Ontario, which in 2015-16 funded 1,676 individual artists and 1,125 organizations in 209 communities across Ontario for a total of $50.5 million. We acknowledge the support of the Canada Council for the Arts, which last year invested $153 million to bring the arts to Canadians throughout the country. This project has been made possible in part by the Government of Canada and with the support of the Ontario Media Development Corporation.

Cover design: Tyler Cleroux
Cover image: iStock

Library and Archives Canada Cataloguing in Publication

McLean, Dirk, 1956-, author
        Team Fugee / Dirk McLean.

Issued in print and electronic formats.
ISBN 978-1-4594-1205-7 (paperback).--ISBN 978-1-4594-1207-1 (epub)

        I. Title.

PS8575.L3894T43 2017   jC813'.54   C2016-906040-3
                                                 C2016-906041-1

Published by: Distributed by:
James Lorimer & Company Ltd.,   Formac Lorimer Books
Publishers   5502 Atlantic Street
117 Peter Street, Suite 304   Halifax, NS, Canada
Toronto, ON, Canada   B3H 1G4
M5V 0M3
www.lorimer.ca

Printed and bound in Canada.
Manufactured by Friesens Corporation in Altona, Manitoba, Canada in January 2017.
Job #229618

For Reneé, Jessica and Melissa.
And my mother, Jacqueline and father, Alonzo.

"He is looking at me, like a brother, a big brother who cannot feel the awful pain but whose compassion is meant to ease it."

Austin Clarke, The Origin of Waves

Contents

Prologue
Leaving Homeland

The scorching Nigerian sun beat down upon the soccer field. Boys in blue shorts and red shorts, all in white T-shirts, were clumped at one end of the field. All of the watching Norfolk Hope Orphanage residents and staff, including kitchen helpers, chanted along with six drummers:

> *You scored once. Ose!*
> *Now score twice. Ose!*
> *Better still, three is nice*
> *Bounce the ball*
> *Bounce the ball. Ose, Ose!*

Eleven-year-old Ozzie, dressed in all-red, crouched in front of the goal.

"One more save in this penalty shootout, then victory will be ours," he muttered to himself. He wiped the sweat from his forehead with his bare arm.

The striker jogged three steps and kicked the dusty,

white ball hard. Ozzie guessed that it was heading to his left. He dived in that direction. But the ball, with a mind of its own, curved and found the right corner of the net.

Silence.

The spectators swarmed the field as the other team celebrated. In fact, everyone celebrated.

Ozzie rose and limped over to pick·up the ball. A car accident when he was little had left him with one leg shorter than the other. Ozzie knew that he still had a lot to learn as a goalkeeper. But after tomorrow it would be in another place, on different soil.

Ozzie's sister, Rebecca, ran up and gave him a big hug. Her short braids tickled Ozzie's neck as she hugged him.

"Nice play, little brother."

"I had fun."

His captain handed him a black marker saying, "Sign, Ozzie. We're retiring this one."

As Ozzie signed the ball he scanned the crowd. Some were friends from the past three years. He held the image in his mind of boys and girls with brilliant smiles, laughing, hollering and high-fiving.

He would miss them all.

The orphanage was on Victoria Island, south of Nigeria's capital city, Lagos. It was made up of four buildings with balconies facing into a square. Ozzie had heard that it had once been a private boarding school. But now, instead of the rich, it was children who had lost their parents to crisis and civil unrest who called it home.

The following morning, in Room 4B of the Boy's Wing, Ozzie unwrapped a purple silk scarf to reveal a book.

"Should I leave it for the library?" he asked Rebecca.

"No. Perhaps one day we will read it," she said as she packed Ozzie's clothes. "It's the only thing we have from our father."

He passed his hand over the cover. There was a crimson stain on it. Then he shook the dust from the scarf, wrapped the scarf around the book and tied a knot.

Rebecca hooked a red and black beaded chain around his neck. He found himself on the verge of crying. He kept his head down so his sister wouldn't see.

"Show me where we are going again," he asked with dark eyes blinking.

"Okay," Rebecca sighed. "But we must get to the Canadian Embassy soon."

Rebecca took two maps from her knapsack and spread them onto his bed. One was a map of Canada they had both had studied closely the past few months. The other one was of the Greater Toronto Area in the province of Ontario.

Ozzie's hand trembled as he pointed to Scarborough where *new* parents were waiting for them.

"What if they don't want us and send us back?"

"Don't worry, Ozzie. We'll be okay," Rebecca reassured him. She rubbed his low-cut hair.

Ozzie did not feel reassured. This was one big change. And though it was one he had looked forward to, he hoped it was the last one. He hated big changes.

1
Incident on the Field

Ozzie cradled a well-used soccer ball as he trotted onto the grassy field at William Hall Public School. He was now thirteen, and was followed by eleven other grade seven and eight Nigerian refugees. They all chanted:

Soccer is our favourite sport
Favourite sport, favourite sport, favourite sport

Ozzie stood in the middle as they formed a circle around him. He dropped the ball to his side and silently led their first stretching exercise.

Suddenly, Victor Bayazid, trailed by the Syrian soccer players, stormed through the circle. Ozzie's and Victor's groups never played against each other, only among themselves.

"It's our turn to use the field today," Victor said.

"I don't think so," said Ozzie, straightening up. "Go back and check the schedule," he offered calmly.

"I checked."

"Check again."

"I... did," Victor said, but he did not seem sure. "I checked."

"What, can't you read?" Ozzie chuckled.

Victor's mood darkened. "You all leave... now!" he screamed.

It was a hot September afternoon in third week of the school year. Each group had been allowed twenty-minute sessions on the field to play six-a-side soccer before the school's flag football team began their regular practice. The Nigerians and the Syrians alternated Monday through Thursday with no Fridays. Ozzie had organized his group, who had played through the summer on neighbourhood fields.

"Victor, Victor, what are you going to do, hothead, start a war with us?" Ozzie taunted.

Ozzie's players laughed.

Victor blushed. He shoved Ozzie, who stumbled backwards. As he regained his balance, Ozzie struck Victor with a head-butt. Victor's head snapped back, throwing black hair off his thin face. He grabbed Ozzie's chain. It broke and scattered beads among the blades of grass. Ozzie became enraged.

Both groups, Nigerians and Syrians, all refugees, formed two semicircles around Ozzie and Victor. He and Victor crouched like wrestlers about to dive at each other.

A dark, towering figure rushed in between. His arms were outstretched to keep the two team leaders separated.

"Boys, enough," he said firmly. "There will be no fighting on this field."

It was Mr. Greenidge, the gym teacher. His skin was blue-black, he had a round face, and you saw his prominent cheeks before noticing his calm, dreamy, black eyes. Those eyes were ablaze with accusation as he looked from Ozzie to Victor.

"Victor started it," tall, muscular Ade yelled from Ozzie's side.

"It's our turn!" Muhammad shouted from behind Victor.

"No way!" cried Sunny from behind Ozzie.

Mr. Greenidge held up his arms silencing them all. Before Ozzie or Victor could say anything, he glanced at his clipboard. Then he blew air out of his mouth in a sigh while his eyes bulged. Ozzie thought that Mr. Greenidge looked funny. But he dared not laugh.

"Ozzie, Victor, follow me, please," said Mr. Greenidge. "The rest of you may go home. No soccer today for anyone."

"My beads," said Ozzie, looking at the grass.

"Don't worry, Ozzie, we'll find them," Ade promised.

⚽ ⚽ ⚽

The three arrived at Principal Jenny Arsenault's office as she was locking the door. She carried a purse and a laptop case and wheeled a briefcase.

Principal Arsenault was athletically tall with shiny black hair and green eyes. Ozzie had asked his dad about the school he would be attending. So he knew that the old school here had been saved from closure by the arrival of various refugees to the area. The principal had come to run the newly opened school, still named William Hall Public School, after a Black Nova Scotian who fought in World War I and was awarded the Victoria Cross for bravery.

"If this can't wait until tomorrow, walk with me," she said.

As they hurried along the main hall, Mr. Greenidge explained what had happened on the field.

"After checking my clipboard I realized that the mistake was mine and mine alone," admitted the gym teacher. "Ozzie and Victor, I apologize to both of you for mixing up the sessions. But I knew that the incident had to be reported to you, Principal Arsenault."

He pushed open the side door. They all stepped into the yard and headed toward the parking lot.

"I appreciate your apology, Mr. Greenidge. And the fact that you volunteered to coordinate two groups of students who wanted to enjoy their sport," she said.

"However, there is absolutely no reason for the two of you to resort to physical assault."

Both boys looked at the ground.

"I am sorry that there isn't a proper soccer program at this school," she continued. "We are still in a re-building phase."

Principal Arsenault started walking again. She aimed her key at a green Volvo. The door unlocked and the car started.

"Ozzie and Victor, I'd like you to apologize to each other," she said, standing next to her car.

"I didn't start it," said Ozzie, looking at Victor.

Victor looked at Principal Arsenault. She looked at her watch. Both Ozzie and Victor remained silent.

"Fine. I have to rush to a meeting. You boys have the evening to think it over. Report back to me at eight-fifteen tomorrow morning," she stated. "If you do not apologize to each other, neither group will be allowed to use the field for soccer."

She placed everything in her back seat, waving off Mr. Greenidge's offer of assistance. And she drove off — leaving each of them in their own thoughts.

2
A Decision to Make

Ozzie found taking an interest in his surroundings was a way of feeling at home. Since arriving from Nigeria two years before, Ozzie had learned about local history. What he learned added to his love of history in general. Malvern was a constantly changing community of various races and incomes. There were rich people whose homes dated back to the 1800s, but it was always becoming *more colourful*, Dad would say, as new immigrants found it. Some new arrivals did well. Others struggled, even with government support.

Ozzie, towered over by Ade and large-bodied Josiah, walked up Neilson Road. Ozzie held a tissue wrapped around the beads his friends had recovered from the field.

"Don't wimp out and apologize," said Ade.

"Victor was wrong to push you," Josiah chirped. "He got off lightly. I would have given him one kick, yes."

"Maybe I teased him too much," Ozzie said.

A Decision to Make

"It was Mr. Greenidge's fault. He admitted it like a man. That should be enough," said Ade.

"You're right, Ade. That's why you should face Principal Arsenault tomorrow, not me," Ozzie joked. "Pretend you are me."

"Make sure you get that limp right, or she'll know you are an imposter," Josiah added.

They fell into laughter as they crossed the tiny bridge over the tracks. Below, a GO train sped commuters toward their homes from downtown Toronto. That train did not stop in this area. Ozzie had read about how Scarborough residents felt that they were treated like orphans by the city. He spent a lot of time in the library, especially on Saturday mornings, and would often get librarians to fill in gaps in the facts he got from the Internet.

As they neared their homes, the boys knocked fists together, saying their goodbyes. Ade and Josiah lived in the same co-op. They had been adopted by neighbouring families around the same time as Ozzie and Rebecca came to live with theirs.

"Tonight Toronto FC is going to give the Vancouver Whitecaps a good pounding," Ozzie called out as Ade and Josiah dashed across Neilson Road.

Ozzie tried to focus on the upcoming game, rather than his own problem. Dad had promised that Ozzie could watch the first half of the match if he finished his homework beforehand. Ozzie could watch the recorded second half on the weekend. It was all learning for him, for both teams had goalkeepers who were exciting to watch.

Ozzie lived on a street called Crow's Trail, where everyone knew their neighbours. Every Labour Day weekend there was a community block party called a *Blocko*. In the street, party music blared, children were entertained and food was shared banquet style under huge tents. Ozzie couldn't wait for the next one, even though Labour Day had been only a few weeks ago.

Ozzie walked up to their plain-looking row house. Mom's front garden still boasted a small patch of peonies, daisies and pink roses.

Inside the house, African and Caribbean décor with well-kept ferns, long-stemmed aloe and other, colourful plants greeted him. Ceiling fans instead of air conditioning kept the house cool. Nigeria's popular HighLife music was blaring, a favourite in the home because of Mom's own Nigerian roots. The drum beat transported him to another place and time as the outside world retreated swiftly.

Ozzie removed his running shoes near the front entrance and leaned his backpack against the basement door. He washed his hands in the half-bathroom near the entrance. Then he danced his way into the kitchen. Rebecca, now sixteen, and with long braids, was singing along while she put supper in the oven to warm up. The smell of the spices filled his nostrils, and his belly gurgled in anticipation.

Rebecca gave Ozzie a quick hug. "Taste this," she said, offering him a spoonful of the sauce she was preparing. "For the red snapper."

"Not enough salt," he suggested.

"Salt kills the spices," she replied. "You'll have to live with it."

"Yes, chef."

Ozzie handed her the tissue with the beads. He told her about the incident with Victor and that he might be banished from the field forever. Even if he was banned only for the rest of the year, it would be forever. This was Ozzie's final year at that school, unless he failed and had to repeat Grade eight. They both knew that was never going to happen, since Mom and Dad were strict about school. Proper Education was their middle name.

"Promise me you won't tell Mom and Dad anything," Ozzie pleaded with his sister.

"I promise nothing. If this blows up and they ask if I knew, I won't lie. This is between you and your girlfriend, Principal Arsenault." She smirked.

"Stop it." He blushed. His dark skin did not redden. It simply took on a glow.

"I thought she liked you."

Any answer Ozzie might have made was stopped when Dad arrived in the family's Lexus, home from his job as a social worker. Mom followed, a minute later in her Mini Cooper, from Scarborough Centenary Hospital where she worked as a doctor.

As he entered the kitchen, Dad lowered the music a little. Rebecca did not mind.

"Anything new at school?" Dad asked, rubbing Ozzie's shaved head.

"Same old, same old," Ozzie replied. He looked at Rebecca to see if she would betray him.

"My History teacher keeps complaining that the room is too hot. We think she's going through menopause," Rebecca said.

"Or she could be pregnant," Ozzie said, relieved that the conversation was not about him.

"Well said, Dr. Oz," Dad teased. "Two doctors in the family now. I'll live to 125 with all this health care."

"Let's all eat," said Mom wearily. "I have to go back to the hospital."

"And I have a parent council meeting," Dad added. "You're on your own for the match tonight, Ozzie. Remember, only the first half."

"Fine, Dad," Ozzie beamed.

Mom and Dad had not noticed that he was not wearing his beaded chain.

❁ ❁ ❁

Fifteen minutes into the soccer match, Toronto FC led 1–0. Rebecca came into the living room and tossed the

A Decision to Make

restrung beaded chain to Ozzie.

"Thanks, Sis. You are the best." he said, slipping the chain around his neck.

"You owe me. And I will collect," she warned.

Rebecca held up a purple scarf. Ozzie recognized it and what it was wrapped around...

The book, he thought. *Our father's favourite book.*

"I'm going to start reading this now." She smiled and headed to the basement.

Ozzie nodded. He picked up his cell phone and speed-dialled his best friend.

"Dylan Michael Gabriel Uriel Hollingsworth," Ozzie said to the voice who answered. "Are you watching?"

"Yeah, Ousmane Ocala Holder. I think the Whitecaps will come back strong. They're always better in the second half," Dylan replied.

"That's what I'm afraid of. Toronto FC could be lulled into false security."

Taking breaks to watch the game, Ozzie told Dylan about the incident with Victor. "What do you think I should do?" he asked.

"If I was you, and I'm glad I'm not you, I would not want to be in this situation, with it being only September and all. A balmy September at that..."

"... get to the point."

"Sorry, Ozzie. Rambling on is a Welsh trait from my dad. I'm trying to shake it."

"You can't help it. So?"

"Say you're sorry. Beg for the royal court's mercy. Promise you'll never head-butt any of Her Majesty Queen Jenny's subjects again, even if the jerk pushes you first."

"What if I apologize and Victor doesn't? Won't I look like a wuss?"

"Nah, Victor would look like the weakling. Keep in mind, Her Majesty likes to hand out suspensions like red cards at the World Cup."

"Okay, I'll think it over. And over. Thanks, Dylan."

The Whitecaps scored. It was an equalizer. The score became 1-1.

"Nooo!" screamed Dylan.

"Toronto FC didn't see it coming."

"I've seen enough. Gotta go."

"Good luck with your cross-country meet tomorrow, Dylan."

They both hung up. Ozzie sat staring at the screen, but his mind was on anything but the match. He liked hearing his full surname — Ocala from his birth parents, and Holder from his adopted parents, who had come to Canada from Trinidad & Tobago. His birth father used to say, "A good name is better than gold." Ozzie had double gold. When he and Rebecca first arrived some children at school mimicked his accent and asked him to roar like a lion. But he was proud of all his names and what they said about him.

He decided to read for half an hour before bed.

A Decision to Make

Ozzie's latest novel was *Mella and the N'anga* by Gail Nyoka. After his thoughts about his name, the book would take his mind to ancient Africa. But his mind kept travelling right back home to the decision he had to make.

If only my school had a proper soccer program, he thought. *I wouldn't be in this mess.*

3
Ozzie United

It was another sunny morning. Ozzie had risen early and still didn't know what he was going to do. He arrived at school looking smart with his white, crested polo shirt tucked into black trousers. He entered the office reception area at eight-fifteen, seconds before Victor. The office secretary told the boys to sit and wait. Principal Arsenault's office door was closed. Ozzie and Victor avoided looking at each other.

Ozzie closed his eyes to block out his surroundings. It was only then that he realized he was nervous. He opened his eyes when he heard a door squeak open.

"Ozzie and Victor, good morning. Please come in," Mr. Greenidge said as if he was inviting them in for breakfast.

On entering, Ozzie saw Principal Arsenault sitting erect behind her desk. He thought of Dylan's constant referral to her as Her Majesty. She did look sort of majestic in a gold power suit.

The boys were not invited to sit.

"Victor, I'm sorry I teased you," Ozzie blurted out before anyone said anything. He surprised himself as he heard his words echo in the room.

Victor looked like Ozzie had slapped him awake from a deep sleep. "Ozzie, sorry... for pushing you..."

Principal Arsenault and Mr. Greenidge looked at each other. It seemed to Ozzie that they were silently scrambling to come up with a Plan B.

"Do either of you recall what this month's character word is?" the principal asked.

After a few seconds of quiet both Ozzie and Victor said, "Respectfulness," at the same time.

"Good. Normally, an incident like this would lead to suspensions, parents being notified, tears even. Your apologies show maturity. However, such actions as yours cannot go without consequences," she said and nodded to Mr. Greenidge.

Mr. Greenidge cleared his throat like he was about to give a speech.

"Ozzie and Victor, you and your soccer teams are to play a presentation match in front of the school. It will be on the Friday before Thanksgiving weekend, in two weeks. There will be two twenty-minute halves with a ten-minute break between."

Mr. Greenidge took a coin from his pocket and showed both sides to Ozzie and Victor. He pointed to Victor.

"Heads. I mean tails," called Victor.

"Make up your mind," said Mr. Greenidge.

"Heads," Victor said once more.

Mr. Greenidge tossed the coin high. It almost touched the ceiling before falling again.

Dad always says that in the law of averages heads wins most often, Ozzie thought. *Why didn't I get to choose? And what's the prize anyway?*

Mr. Greenidge caught the coin and slammed it on top of Principal Arsenault's desk for all to see. It was heads.

"Practices on the field thirty minutes before school each morning or thirty minutes at lunchtime. Victor?"

Victor quickly said, "Lunchtime."

All right. I still have lunchtime to do some homework, thought Ozzie.

"The after-school sessions will continue as before. No mistakes, I promise," concluded Mr. Greenidge, looking toward Principal Arsenault.

"Any questions, boys?" she asked.

Will there be a trophy? Will the school band play? Will Major League Soccer scouts attend? Ozzie asked silently.

But when no questions were asked aloud, Principal Arsenault stood up. "Respectfulness. Don't make me regret this," she said sternly.

Minutes later in homeroom, Ozzie and Victor sat further away from each other than before. Battle lines had been drawn. The class stood for the playing of "O Canada" over the PA system. It was an upbeat rendition by a group of Cree singers. Ozzie never knew which of five different versions they would hear. It could be sung by the soulful R&B singer or even the French operatic tenor.

After a series of announcements, Principal Arsenault declared the first soccer match at William Hall PS as the beginning of a new era of the school. The whole class erupted in chatter. Dylan, sitting beside Ozzie, turned and high-fived him.

"The first in Her Majesty's reign, she means," Dylan smirked. "If that's her new version of consequences, I'd better think up some trouble."

Ozzie liked early mornings. The question was would the rest of his team feel the same way?

⚽ ⚽ ⚽

At lunchtime Ozzie and his team met in an empty, unlocked classroom on the second floor. There was only a teacher's desk and some chairs. Cobwebs hung from the ceiling. It hadn't seen a broom in a long time. Ozzie recalled that the orphanage in Nigeria used every room.

While they ate, Ozzie shared the details of the presentation match with his friends. He imitated Mr. Greenidge with a slight Trinidad & Tobago accent.

"In conclusion, all-you better put on a good-good

display of soccer talent, or it's my ass on de line," Ozzie said to giggles.

"Does that mean your supposed suspensions are supposedly suspended?" asked Sunny, shaking his mop of hair.

That sent the rest of the team into more laughter.

"No suspensions," said Ozzie. "Let's get serious. We need a captain. I nominate Ade."

"I nominate Ozzie," said Ade.

"Ozzie, you have been organizing us all along, it makes sense... Captain," said Sunny. "I second that."

"All in favour?" asked Ade.

Everyone, except Ozzie, raised their hand.

"It's settled," stated Ade. "Now for the next order of business, Captain."

"Okay, men, I'll lead you into battle. It will be fierce. It will be bloody. It may be muddy. Some of you will not come out alive. Just don't call me Captain, again," said Ozzie, talking tough like some action-movie star. He was not sure which one.

"What about a name? We can't just be Ozzie's team," said Peter, a sandy-headed grade seven student with his mouth full of sandwich. "And I want a midfielder spot."

"Manchester United is already spoken for. Scarborough United doesn't have the right ring. The only logical choice is Ozzie United." Ade beamed. "All in favour?"

All hands raised, and Ozzie said, "Dis... missed."

"Aye, aye, aye, Captain," they chanted.

Ozzie smiled, despite himself.

That afternoon, with the field to themselves, Ozzie United held their first practice. Ozzie led them through a quick stretch. For fifteen minutes they executed a drill, with everyone taking turns kicking penalty shots on goalkeeper Ozzie. Ozzie dived to the left and to the right, getting up quickly. He jumped up and caught balls, hugging them into his chest. He also watched balls speed past him. He caught the last ball and brought them all into a circle.

"Good practice, guys." He smiled. "If you are ever in that position, don't let the goalkeeper see you look at where you are going to shoot the ball."

Ozzie walked home alone. He realized that he had to start thinking like a coach. He would have to plan only a few drills. Too many would be boring for the team. He would concentrate on activities and tactics. He had eleven players to place. Ten players would be divided into three forwards, four midfielders and three defenders. That left one substitute. Kenneth had been the other goalkeeper, but he could also play any other position.

Each player would practice actions on their own. They would practice dribbling — moving the ball along the field lightly with their toe or the inside of the foot. They would learn heading — throwing the ball in the air and striking it with their forehead. They would kick the ball against a wall from a distance.

That evening Ozzie, Rebecca and Dad gathered for supper. Mom had to work late. Ozzie shared his news. But he did not say how the presentation match came about.

"Your principal sure is mercurial," Dad said, munching some salad.

"What's mercurial?" asked Ozzie.

"She's full of mercury." Rebecca smirked.

"Rebecca..." Dad said in mock sternness. "Ozzie, it means she seems to change her opinions quickly. One minute she prefers girls' volleyball over soccer. Now she's pushing soccer. Our parent council has been trying to get soccer back into your school since last spring. And now this all of a sudden."

"We're not official school teams, Dad. Only a... a little showcase. Victor and the Syrians have been playing for fun... like Ade and the rest of us. No big thing." He glanced at Rebecca hoping she would not add the truth to the conversation.

"Will Auntie Lisa and Uncle Russell be coming this Thanksgiving?" Ozzie asked. He hoped changing the subject would keep Dad from asking more questions. Auntie Lisa was Dad's sister and they lived north of Toronto near Barrie.

"I believe so," Dad replied.

"Tell her to bake *two* whole salmons this time. On that wood thing."

"A cedar plank. I'll give her your order," Dad chuckled.

"With maple-mustard glaze."

"That, too. Anything else?"

"No, Dad. Great meal, Rebecca," Ozzie said, standing up to leave the table before the soccer game came up again.

4
Training Begins

The morning started with Ozzie waking up extra early. Six o'clock. He had written "OZZIE UNITED" on the inside cover of a new hard-cover notebook that he had kept for a special occasion. He then wrote out an activity for his team to play out on the field. The entire team was to imagine they were making a charge against Victor's team:

The goalkeeper kicks the ball easily to a nearby defender. He passes it across to another defender beside him, who passes the ball high over to the third defender. Left defender traps the ball before it goes over the outside left line, stopping the action. He looks ahead for a midfielder. The four midfielders are almost bunched together. Not a good sign. Who to send the ball to? Left full defender kicks the ball over to the right defender who heads it to a centre midfielder. He traps it with his chest, letting it roll to the ground and stops it with his foot. He turns around and kicks it to the left midfielder who seems to move toward the left corner area. But he changes his mind when he spots the right midfielder alone. He kicks the ball over there, making sure that the ball does not touch his hands and cause a penalty. Right midfielder sees the line of the opposition's defence ahead. If he is afraid of them it does not show. In the meantime the other three midfielders dart toward those two mean-looking defenders in front of the goal line. The right midfielder sends the ball toward the middle. One of the two centre midfielders jumps higher than everyone else. He heads the ball past the defenders, past the goalkeeper, into the back corner of the net. Goal!

Ozzie called out the plays like that in his head from his bird's-eye view from the goal. It also helped him to stay alert. Ozzie waved everyone over to him. They formed a wide circle around him.

"You did well today, guys," Ozzie said. "How did it feel?"

"Tough," Josiah panted, still catching his breath.

"How so?" asked Ozzie.

"They were invisible," Josiah said.

"No matter. I'm ready for Victor's team. I say bring them on now," Peter boasted.

"What kind of activity was that anyway, Ozzie?" Ade asked.

Ozzie looked around at everyone's faces before he responded. "We have only ever played six-a-side against each other. I wanted you to get the feeling of playing like a full team against a single opponent."

"Single? There were eleven of them. And sometimes I couldn't tell where they all were — they were all over the field," Kenneth said, to much laughter and talking all around. None of them had ever seen an activity like that before.

Ozzie broke into the chatter. "Now, I didn't say this before and I don't want to say it again. Kenneth and Ezekiel, you were four minutes late for practice." He raised a hand, silencing them. "No excuses. We only have two weeks. If you can't wake up on time, let me know and I'll call your house and wake you up."

"Spoken like a true coach," Ade said.

The team widened the circle. For the last five minutes of their time, they kicked the ball across to each other, calling out the team member's name beforehand.

⚽ ⚽ ⚽

Friday night, Ozzie and Rebecca had the run of the house. Mom and Dad were out on a date. That morning Ozzie had overheard Mom saying that she felt stuck in her job.

Rebecca and her girlfriends had taken over the basement. Indra was of Guyanese heritage and Fola, Nigerian. They headed down to enjoy their mini film festival.

Ozzie and Dylan settled into the living room with the West Indian *roti* they both loved. He remembered explaining it to Dylan. The wrapper was flatter than a pancake, much larger and folded in a way to keep the curried filling inside. It was delicious!

The boys turned on the TV just in time to hear the opening whistle for the European Cup playoff match between Ireland and Ukraine.

"Ireland has been playing well these days," said Dylan, biting into his goat roti.

Ozzie chewed some of his vegetarian roti filling. "Don't rule out Ukraine. They're playing smarter than last year. France, too."

They clicked bottles of Malta Carib and drank, grinning like millionaires and enjoying the malt flavoured beverage. By halftime the score was still 0–0, despite both Irish and Ukrainian goalkeepers having saved amazing shots.

"This match is all defensive," commented Dylan. "When you coach your boys, get them to score. Scoring wins matches," he advised.

"I'll remember that," said Ozzie, smiling.

That night, before falling asleep, Ozzie thought about a save by the Irish goalkeeper. He had rushed forward and caught the ball instead of waiting for it to come to him. Forward thinking!

The first Saturday of fall still felt like summer to Ozzie as he completed his chores. He was happy that the girls had tidied up the basement after their partying. He did not have much to do there.

Ozzie rushed off to Malvern Public Library. Ozzie

found it the perfect place to complete weekend assignments and learn more about local history. Its high, open ceilings gave Ozzie the feeling of space like the Anglican Church that Mom and Dad took him and Rebecca to sometimes. The main desk with helpful librarians faced the entrance. To the left of the desk was a teens' section he was finally allowed to explore now that he was no longer restricted to the children's collection. A presentation area with a large bay window allowed the morning sun to stream through.

Who's that? Ozzie wondered. He thought that he saw Victor going into one of the meeting rooms beyond the books in other languages off to the right. *Now, that is probably my mind trying to trick me because he is my opponent*, he thought. He slid into a booth in the quiet study area behind the English as a Second Language stacks.

That afternoon the Ozzie United practice was on the small soccer field at Blessed Mother Teresa Catholic Secondary School, just to the east of the library. Usually it was occupied by older teens. Ozzie felt lucky to have the field and that it was so close.

"Today we work on the *corner kick*," Ozzie said, putting aside his notebook. "It's one of the easiest ways for a team to score a goal. When the other team is awarded a corner kick, the goalkeeper gets his team, including the three main defenders — Peter, Josiah and Owen — to cover each opponent in the area in front of the goal. They must prevent the ball from going into their net. In this case, my net."

Forward Sam stood on the corner arc left of the goal with Ade on the right. They waited for Ozzie to settle on the goal line. The others formed the opposition, sending the ball toward the middle front of the goal so their teammate could score.

After a few corner kicks from each side, Sam stopped the action.

"I should be on the right corner, Ozzie," he complained. "I shoot better that way."

"You never get to choose which corner you shoot from," Ade shouted, moving toward the centre.

"Let's switch sides," Sam yelled back, running to meet Ade.

"Guys, it's only a simple activity. In a real match neither of you might win the corner. It might be a midfielder."

"But, Ozzie..." Sam started again.

"Tell you what, ten more kicks each from your corners, then switch. Afterwards, the midfielders will get a turn. Back to positions, everyone," he ordered.

While walking home, Ozzie thought about the practice. He hoped the team would play well and not end up fighting each other in front of the school to embarrass him, Principal Arsenault and Mr. Greenidge. Something about the team wasn't right. He could not quite place it.

He went home and watched the second half of the Toronto FC versus the Whitecaps game from earlier in the week. He already knew that Toronto FC had won by a slim 3–2 in a penalty shootout. But he wanted to see what he could learn to pass on to his team. *His team?* A lot had happened that week. A week ago he simply got some guys together for soccer. Now he was the captain of a full team with a big match looming and a principal who hoped she had not made a mistake.

5
Guards and Spies

Passing by the athletic office during lunch, Ozzie spotted the revised field schedule posted on the notice board. Victor United had the field after school. Their name seemed appropriate, he thought, for he and Victor had both united their teams. Ozzie now had to show which one was the strongest team.

It wasn't just local history Ozzie liked. He also enjoyed books and stories about castles, kings, queens and knights. In the unused classroom, he completed a diagram on the board with a marker. Ozzie United straggled in and began grumbling.

"What's he done now?"

"What are these words?"

"You're the one who said he should be captain."

"Okay, fellas, this won't take long," said Ozzie, pointing at what was clearly the goal. "This is the main gate to the castle, or keep. As goalkeeper, I am the final protector of the castle."

"Who's in the castle?" Josiah asked.

"The queen, of course. We're Queen Jenny's special guards. We keep the keep safe."

"Yeah, right..." a voice snickered.

"No interruptions, guys," Ade barked.

"In front of me is a wide bridge," continued Ozzie. "On the bridge are three of the fiercest defenders in the kingdom. Josiah, Owen and Cyril. Kenneth, you too, for now."

"That's why you can't be late for practice, Josiah," chided Sunny.

"Beyond the bridge in a clearing in the forest are four more guards, midfielders. Peter, Atah, Ezekiel and Sunny." Ozzie pointed to the areas on his drawing. "Beyond the clearing is the border, the centre line."

"It's where the queen's land ends," said Josiah.

"Exactly!" Ozzie was getting excited. "It's the first line of defence and the first line of offence. It requires three of the most highly trained warriors. Sometimes they will take the four midfielders with them across the border into enemy territory, where they will..."

"Score for queen and realm!" shouted Sunny.

He looked at his final team in their positions and tossed the ball to Ade.

⚽ ⚽ ⚽

Guards and Spies

Ozzie centred the following morning's practice on an attacking drill. Rain had fallen the evening before. The school's field was moist, but not soggy.

The point of the drill was to move the ball from the middle line toward the opposing goal area. It involved the four midfielders and the two forwards working together. With each exercise they tried to get the ball in front of the goal for scoring or aimed for one of the corners first to win the corner for a kick.

During the drill, Ozzie spotted Muhammad. He seemed to be watching them and writing on a piece of paper. Ozzie had seen Mr. Greenidge observing their morning practices from a distance. That was okay. He probably did that for Victor United as well, for he was not allowed to coach either team. But what was not okay was Muhammad spying on them and taking notes.

Ozzie could not share the information with his team, fearing a possible fight. But at lunchtime he watched Victor United's practice. He noted how they moved the ball between them and communicated their play as if reading each other's thoughts. Some of them had sharp moves. But they seemed to move in slow motion like they had all the time in the world.

When the practice ended Victor ran toward Ozzie. Ozzie was surprised to be caught out. Victor had not looked in his direction once during the practice.

"Looking for secret tips, Ozzie?"

"I'm only doing what you sent Muhammad to do this morning — spy on the enemy."

"I did nothing. If he watched your silly training, it was his choosing. I did not order him."

"Tell him to stop."

"I tell him nothing. But I ask him, as favour, not to do it. But only if you... or your little boys... stop spying on us."

"Okay then," said Ozzie, walking away from Victor.

The next day, when the lunch buzzer sounded, four of the Victor Uniteds headed toward a few Ozzie Uniteds in the hallway. Ezekiel started a quiet chant which Peter and Sunny picked up on:

> *Victor's boys, say you're sorry*
> *Victor's boys, you are posers*
> *Victor's boys, don't you worry*
> *Victor's boys, you're just losers*

The four Victor Uniteds, led by Muhammad, stopped in front of them and replied:

> *Nigerians can't play soccer*
> *Nigerians better quit*
> *Nigerians why you bother*
> *Our Victor United team is it*

Both teams used lots of hand gestures as they chanted at the same time to drown each other out. Soon they drew a crowd. Ozzie was about to step in when a teacher said,

"Okay, that's enough. Move along, students."

The boys ignored her.

"Move along. Or you go to the office!" she barked, stepping between them, unafraid.

The teams walked away from each other. Ozzie thought about the names he had been called as an African. He thought about the teasing his limp had caused. *No, I did not fall out of a tree in the jungle.*

The next day Mr. Greenidge summoned Ozzie and Victor to a meeting in Ozzie United's room.

"Sit," Mr. Greenidge ordered. Ozzie and Victor sat cautiously.

"I have observed you and your teams — your behaviour. How you react to each other around the school," he said. He was clearly upset. "You two are supposed to be leaders." He started pacing the floor. "Stop the nonsense *now*. I don't care who started what. Next week is your presentation match in front of the school. It is not a grudge match. That's not good sportsmanship."

He wiped the edge of the desk with a tissue and looked at the boys, almost sadly. His tone became softer.

"What your school and Principal Arsenault want to see is a display of your skills and abilities. Soccer is something you both love, right?"

"All my life, Mr. Greenidge," said Ozzie.

"Yes. That's right," Victor offered.

"There cannot be enmity between both of you and your teams. Keep this a healthy competition. Can you do that?"

Both nodded.

"And pass this on to your teammates. If you all cannot be civil toward each other, the presentation match will be called off. Understood?" Both Ozzie and Victor bobbed their heads.

"Right. Shake hands like the gentlemen I know you both are," Mr. Greenidge concluded.

Ozzie stuck out his hand and Victor shook it.

As Victor left the room, Mr. Greenidge stopped Ozzie.

"I'm curious, what was the moment when you decided to be a goalkeeper?"

Ozzie thought about it for a few seconds before answering. "I was around nine. Tired of guys making fun of me with my limp, you know? One day the usual goalkeeper for our side at the orphanage was sick. Nobody wanted to go in goal. I walked in for the first time. I'd never thought of that position before. I was hit in the face by the ball and caught it as it bounced off my face. That was the moment. Yeah."

"What happened when the guy came back?"

"They voted him out. They said that if I could take a hit like that and keep playing, I was their man. Your turn. What was the moment you decided to be a gym teacher?"

"I didn't have a moment. I tried out for the Soca Warriors back in Trinidad & Tobago and didn't make the squad. I came here for university and drifted into teaching. I started at Islington PS in the west end. Then Principal Arsenault asked me to come here."

"And you play soccer every Sunday with some fellas."

"How did you know that?" he asked, surprised.

"People talk, Mr. Greenidge. It's a small school. How did you find Ozzie United's room?"

"It's a small school," Mr. Greenidge said. "People talk."

⚽ ⚽ ⚽

October began with overcast skies. Ozzie United had finished their practice before any rain fell.

Walking off the field, Ozzie saw Riad and Ahmed, Victor United defenders. They were struggling to pump their ball at the side of the school. Ozzie smirked to himself. Then he recalled Mr. Greenidge's remarks from the day before.

Ozzie fetched the pump from his locker and ran back to Riad and Ahmed. "That pump is broken. Use this," said Ozzie, handing over his pump.

Riad and Ahmed both looked at Ozzie with wide

eyes. He could tell they were wondering what he was up to.

"Just give it back to me at lunch," Ozzie said.

"Thanks," said Ahmed, taking the pump.

Ozzie turned and walked away before anything further was said.

During the morning announcements Principal Arsenault reminded the school of the presentation match. She also mentioned the character word for October — *Cooperation*. Ozzie smiled to himself.

6
Changes Coming

That evening the full Holder clan gathered for supper. "*Darlings*, I have some news," Mom started. "I had an interview last Friday in Hamilton."

Right away, Ozzie's brain began spinning. "How far is Hamilton from here?" he asked.

"Let Mom finish," Rebecca scolded.

"Roughly one-and-a-half hour's drive," Mom replied. "I have been offered Head of Paediatrics at a new hospital there."

"A promotion with an increase in pay and great benefits," Dad enthused. It sounded as if he was selling something to Ozzie and Rebecca.

"Congratulations, Mom." Rebecca smiled.

"Yes, congratulations, Mom," Ozzie repeated. He couldn't make himself smile. "That's a long drive to work and back."

"Well... we will all have to move," Mom said.

Ozzie and Rebecca stopped eating.

"I will commute Monday to Thursday with earlier

hours. And work from home on Fridays," Dad said.

You're selling what you and Mom had planned all along, Ozzie thought. *That's what grown-ups do. Don't say we have to pack up this weekend.*

"When?"

"I would start the first of December," Mom replied.

Eight weeks away, Ozzie calculated. He thought about what he knew about Mom and Dad before they had become Mom and Dad. Mom had told them that they bought this two-bedroom house intending to have a child. But they were unable to have any of their own. Then they became part of a community group who sponsored orphaned refugees. They had chosen Rebecca and Ozzie to be their children and live in the house.

"I have friends here I like. I just started Grade eleven. Can I commute with you, Dad?" Rebecca pleaded.

"That won't be a good idea, sweetheart," he answered.

"Look, I still have to decide," said Mom. "I haven't said yes. And I haven't quit my job here."

Rebecca excused herself and headed upstairs. Ozzie did not think it would be fair to Mom if he ran off, too.

"Please finish your supper, Ozzie," Mom urged.

He obeyed, chewing slower than he usually did.

Later, in their bedroom, Ozzie and Rebecca sat on her bed. The bedroom's decorations were split down the middle. Rebecca's side had bright cushions and included posters of Drake and Rihanna. Ozzie's side was a combination of Toronto FC, Nigeria's Super Eagles and Manchester United, with a Nigerian HighLife music poster to mix it up a bit. The cream colour of the walls was the only thing that matched.

"Dylan and my soccer buddies are all here," Ozzie said.

"Yeah, I know," said Rebecca. She had calmed down after leaving the dinner table. "New schools. New friends. We've done it before, Ozzie."

"I thought after we came to Canada there would be no more big changes."

"Let's talk to Mom and Dad in the morning."

They spent a few minutes planning what they might say. Then they sat in silence, not sure their plan could work.

Suddenly Rebecca said, "Wanna play memory game?"

That was what she and Ozzie called a game of images they played when they needed to reconnect with their Nigerian roots.

"I'll start," Rebecca said. "Dog peeing on Miss Lemon's oranges in Oja Oba market."

"Smiles on the children's faces whenever Super Eagles scored."

"Swimming in the sea at low tide."

"Calabar Carnival before Christmas."

"The smell of the earth on the first day of the rainy season."

"Field trip to the shrine at Osun Festival in Oshogbo."

As always, the memory game worked. Finally, Ozzie and Rebecca were smiling. They hugged, then got ready for bed.

⚽⚽⚽

"Ozzie... Ozzie... wake up..." Rebecca says in hushed tones.

"What, Sis..."

"Put your things in this bag. We have to leave."

Ozzie rolls out of his cot and steps onto the rug. Moonlight filters through the room.

"Quickly. We must hurry."

Ozzie realizes that Rebecca is frightened, like the morning a few weeks ago when they woke to find their parents gone. Disappeared. And a small trail of blood. One of his teachers had also disappeared the year before. He starts to grab his belongings. The last thing he sees is a book, alone on the table. Rebecca hands him a purple scarf. He wraps the book in it and stuffs it into a leather weekend bag. Rebecca is filling a bag with her own things, but leaving precious items out.

"Put on your shoes, Ozzie. Don't turn on any lights."

They creep down to the main floor of the house

and dash outside. They cram into the back seat of a car with family members Ozzie barely knows. They drive through the darkness, stopping at police checks where he is told to keep silent. At times they stop and wait. Ozzie wonders where they are all going. Before he can ask he feels his eyes closing.

When Ozzie's eyes open, Rebecca is dragging him out of the car. The air is salty. It is early morning. Noisy birds fly overhead. He and Rebecca watch the car drive away. They stand with their bags on the ground. Looking at the huge door in front of them, he sees a word he will come to know as "orphanage." This is to be their new home.

⚽⚽⚽

Ozzie woke up mumbling, "Orphanage. Orphanage..."

He had not had that dream in a long time.

The Holder household was getting ready for school and work.

Ozzie and Rebecca had called their summit. They were ready to state their case for the family to remain in Scarborough. Ozzie swallowed the last of his oatmeal while Rebecca munched on a wedge of apple.

"Mom and Dad, you both grew up in this neighbourhood," Ozzie started.

"Ozzie and I know first-hand how traumatic it can be to leave a home environment," Rebecca continued.

She aimed to hit an emotional nerve.

Mom and Dad listened, occasionally nodding, sometimes shaking their heads from side to side.

"I'll think about that."

"Umm hmmm..."

"Good point."

"I am not thinking only about my career. I want what's best for the whole family," Mom said, sipping her green tea.

"People, we all have places to get to. Let's discuss this further another time," Dad said. And that brought the summit to a close without a definite decision.

"One more thing. Rebecca and Ozzie, let's keep this a family secret for now," Mom said.

Ozzie and Rebecca smiled at each other. They had scored some points.

Ozzie dashed to his practice. He had to make it on time. After all, he had to keep leading by example.

7
The Spirit of Cooperation

The nets were in place on Blessed Mother Teresa school's soccer field, though the field was smaller than the one at William Hall. Ozzie had decided to hold a six-a-side match for their Saturday afternoon practice. They were going to play forty minutes straight without a break. Dylan had delayed his cross-country practice run to act as referee. He was wearing a black T-shirt with a new dollar-store whistle around his neck.

Ozzie wasn't wearing his beaded chain. No jewellery would be allowed on match day. He felt almost naked without it. He stood in goal. Cyril was defender. Midfielders were Ezekiel and Peter. Ade and Sam stood as forwards. On the opposite end, Kenneth stood in goal with Josiah as defender. Sunny and Atah were midfielders. Forwards were Trevor and Owen.

Standing slightly off centre, Dylan blew the whistle. He had to do it twice because the first time it barely sounded. Ozzie's mental commentary started:

Owen passes the ball to Trevor and crosses into my half of the field. Ade covers him. Sam moves to prevent Owen from getting the ball back. Sunny and Atah trot toward the centre line. Ade steals the ball from Trevor and looks to send the ball over to Sam. Owen is in a better position, blocking Sam instead of Sam blocking him. Ezekiel moves up to help Ade, and they pass the ball between them. Ezekiel runs ahead. Defender Josiah comes forward, looking unsure about whether to defend against Ezekiel or Ade. Ade still has the ball. Josiah focuses on him. Ade appears to head straight toward Josiah. He does not see Ezekiel move past him. Ade lobs the ball above Josiah's head, and Ezekiel heads the ball past goalkeeper Kenneth into the back of the net.

Score! Whistle!

"Offside!" yelled Dylan.

"What?" Ezekiel asked, amazed.

"The goal will not be allowed," Dylan insisted.

"You're blind or what?"

"If you insult me again I'll issue a yellow card," Dylan challenged.

Ade joined Ezekiel. "What kind of ref are you?" asked Ade.

Everyone joined in, ready to add their opinions. They all knew Dylan. He had played with them in the summer. He substituted for either side for six-a-side. But today he was not really one of them. He was the ref.

"I'm warning you too, Ade," Dylan said, taking out some yellow squares of paper.

"Ref, it's not the World Cup..." Sunny said, trying to lighten the mood.

Ozzie couldn't stay silent. "You were offside, Ezekiel."

"Excuse me, goalkeeper, you were way on the opposite side," Ezekiel stated.

"I could still see clearly. Technically, you were over that line. Okay, let's start at the centre again."

Nobody moved.

"Now, guys. Time is precious," said Ozzie. "Dylan, reset your watch."

Everyone returned to their starting positions. Secretly, Ozzie was pleased that the players were taking the play so seriously. He would not want anyone being yellow carded or red carded at the presentation match.

Dylan blew the final whistle as his watch alarm went off. Unlike in pro matches, there were no additional minutes for stoppage. Kenneth's side celebrated a 2–1 victory. Ozzie's side slumped to the ground. All were exhausted. They sat in a circle on the field, even Dylan. Ozzie hooked his beaded chain around his neck, feeling like himself once more.

"Guys, a round of applause for our volunteer referee, Dylan Hollingsworth," Ozzie said. "Thanks for helping us out."

Dylan stood up and bowed, soaking in the cheers of the team and blushing at the same time.

Ozzie went on to explain the reason for the exercise. He had wanted to see how well they were playing together, the communication between midfielders, between forwards and between midfielders and forwards.

"I liked most of what I saw," Ozzie started. "And I'm happy with the way the drills and activities are paying off in such a short time."

Then he explained where they could improve in the coming week.

The two goals scored against him by Trevor and Atah had surprised Ozzie. He knew that next week's practice must include him facing lots of shots. He needed to be sharper.

⚽ ⚽ ⚽

The rest of the team went off to their lives. But Ozzie's afternoon was far from over. He had to live up to his end of a bargain. Dylan was a top-ten cross-country runner in his division. He loved running more than any sport. Ice hockey was only a distant second.

Ozzie joined Dylan for a three-mile run, ending at Malvern Town Centre's east side parking lot. As they cooled down by stretching, Ozzie's thoughts turned again to his home situation.

"Dylan, how do you cope with change?" Ozzie

asked. Remembering Mom's request to keep the family secret, he pretended that his question was coming out of the blue.

Dylan looked at him strangely. "Same as everyone else, I convert it into larger bills so I don't have to carry around all that weight." His face looked serious, but there was a twinkle in his eye.

"You are such an ass, my friend. I mean change, real change."

"Look around, Ozzie. Everything in life is about change. That traffic light we went through just changed. Day changes into night and back again."

"Stop."

"Okay, okay. I cope with change by accepting it."

"Accepting is your solution?"

"I change what I can change. The rest I accept. You're such a deep thinker all of a sudden. What's up?"

"I dunno."

"You're doing fine as a captain. It suits you. Stop worrying. Whatever happens Friday happens."

"It's not the World Cup," they both said together and chuckled.

Ozzie could not say that the real change he was concerned about was not soccer. It was something much bigger and life changing.

⚽ ⚽ ⚽

Indian summer arrived in the second week of October. The heat wave was perfect for outdoor soccer. Wednesday, however, brought warm rain all day. Outdoor practices for both teams were cancelled. Mr. Greenidge secured the gym, but Ozzie United and Victor United had to share the same time period. Ozzie realized that he would not be able to run his intended drill. He signalled for his team to follow him.

"Victor, why don't we all do a couple of drills together?" Ozzie said, approaching the other captain.

"And why would we do that?" Victor asked suspiciously.

Ozzie prayed that his team would not start objecting. They remained silent.

"If we tried to work separately, it would be awkward," Ozzie reasoned.

"Awkward for you, maybe," Victor said.

"The gym's small. Our voices are already echoing off the walls. It wouldn't be long before nobody could hear each other."

Victor seemed to be thinking.

Ozzie became impatient. "Forget it," he said bluntly. "I'm not begging you for anything."

"Wait. You are right. What do you have in mind?"

Ozzie laid out eight disc cones down the length of the gym, roughly thirty centimetres apart.

"We hop between discs one foot at a time. Then we hop on both feet," he explained.

"Okay," Victor agreed. "Afterwards we'll use just one disc at either end. Each guy will run from disc to disc only touching with his toe. Two times each."

"Fine," Ozzie agreed. "But we want this as exercise, not competition. Safety first."

The two teams were still wary of each other, but everything went off without any conflict or secrets traded. Ozzie caught Mr. Greenidge observing them near the door.

The day before the match, the morning was warm. The earth was firm.

"Okay," said Ozzie to his team. "This activity is the Wall of Six, sometimes called the Wall of Five when it's only five players. You've seen it but I want you to pay attention anyway."

Ozzie ignored the groans from a few players.

"A player is *fouled* by an opponent just beyond the goal line. Say he was given a shove to the ground or a hand across the face or a shoe to the groin. The 'victim' is awarded a free kick. Six players from the other team form a wall in front of the goalkeeper, at an angle so the goalkeeper can still see the shooter. There's a defender at either end of the wall in case the ball rebounds. I want you guys prepared for this. A skilled shooter can bend the ball above the wall and curve it into the net behind the goalkeeper. Sometimes the shooter is really bad and hits the wall. This is why the players who make up the wall cover... uh, themselves," Ozzie explained, gesturing at his crotch.

"I guess you're telling us this 'cause those guys are bad shooters," Sunny said with a smile.

"No, I'm telling you so you can have children someday and make me godfather."

Ozzie directed the wall, shuffling the players around, receiving shots from the various shooters. The trick would be bringing all the elements together in a match, Ozzie knew.

During the cool-down stretch, Ozzie saw Peter and Ezekiel exchanging looks. Ezekiel jutted out his chin.

"Ozzie, you still haven't told us what we will be wearing with our black shorts," Ade spoke up.

"We will be shirtless. Our bodies will glisten in the sun. All the girls will take selfies with us, sending them viral. And Manchester United will challenge us to a match," Sunny boasted.

"Guys, any T-shirt you wear will be fine," Ozzie said casually.

He hoped that Dad had picked up the package.

8
The Presentation Match

That night, Ozzie thanked Dad for the package and checked the list twice. He went to bed earlier than usual. He closed his eyes, intending to imagine fifty balls from various angles shooting toward him. He caught each one, hugging it to his chest. But he fell asleep before he got to fifty.

Ozzie woke up and looked at his alarm clock at two-fifteen, three-thirty-five, four-forty-four, and when the alarm went off at six a.m. Dad had already laid out breakfast by the time he entered the kitchen. Ozzie ate heartily, knowing that he would need lots of energy.

Dad started singing in a Calypso style:

My boy, the soccer captain
Leader of the Nigerians
Today they playing the Syrians
It is an inner school campaign
When they take to the field, it's fever
Their opponents better run for cover

'Cause is only goal, goal, goal
Is only goal, goal, goal

Ozzie smiled, hoping Dad's prediction would prove right.

"My boy, captain and coach, how do you feel?"

"I wish there was more time," Ozzie said.

"There's never enough time. Look at it this way, the other team had no more time than you did. Just trust that everything you did with your team will come together."

"Okay, Dad." Something still nagged at him.

"And have fun, Ozzie."

Ozzie nodded. Dad offered him a ride to school. But Ozzie wanted to walk instead. He left, carrying his backpack, lunch and the package. During the slow, leisurely walk to school Ozzie realized what had been nagging him. He recalled watching Victor United. And he recalled the way Ozzie United played six-a-side. He knew then that he had a secret weapon.

The final practice did not involve any actual play. Ozzie reminded his team of all the activities and why they were important. And he shared a final tactic. "Guys, we have a secret weapon. It's the element of speed." At the puzzled looks of his team, Ozzie went on to explain. "We're used to playing six-a-side like we have all the time in the world. There's nothing at stake."

"No urgency," Ade offered.

"Exactly. That's how Victor United play also."

"But we can't go at full speed for the whole match," Sam said.

"We'll choose our moments," Ozzie replied.

Then he opened the package. Checking the list of names and sizes, he handed out what was inside. Each player received a new red T-shirt with OZZIE UNITED on the back. The look on the boys' faces made it worth the effort. They were delighted and, for the first time as a team, speechless.

The sun was hot and high in the sky above William Hall PS as Ozzie United walked toward one end of the field. Ozzie brought up the rear in a pale blue T-shirt and shorts. He had removed his beaded chain. It made him feel like he was shedding something old from his past.

Victor United, in yellow T-shirts, was on the opposite end of the field, already warming up. Victor wore moss green.

There were no metal stands for spectators. Instead, a bumpy hill ran along the west side of the field. It was framed by tall evergreens, cedars and a lone maple tree. That was where students sat to watch home games. School custodians were placing folded wooden chairs at the bottom of the hill for staff.

Ozzie ran up the hill. When he turned around his breath was taken away by a beautiful sight. As promised, Mr. Greenidge had had the grass cut and the field marked in white, with a white ring in the middle and boxed lines in front of each goal. Each corner had a small arc for corner kicks. Borrowed nets were attached to the bottom half of the H-shaped football posts. Since arriving at William Hall PS Ozzie had dreamed of playing soccer for this school. Today would be as close as he would get. He felt like crying. No. He had a job to do. He ran down toward his team.

For the next twenty minutes Ozzie United warmed up with stretches in pairs, knee lifts, rabbit hops over disc cones, sidestepping around other cones. Ozzie's warm-up included receiving shots on goal by Ade and Sam. His forwards were not intending to score on Ozzie in front of the gathering students. But they wanted to give him the feel of seeing and catching the ball. Ozzie spotted Dylan and they waved to each other.

"Guys, you know these three rules already," said Ozzie. "I'm instructed to remind you as your captain. Number one: Use your feet only, not your hands. Number two: Stop when the referee blows the whistle. Number three: Kick the ball into the opposite goal. Now, let's have some fun."

At one o'clock Principal Arsenault said a few words of welcome to the spectators.

"Introducing Victor United, captained by Victor Bayazid." She read off each name as the Syrian boys jogged onto the field and took their positions. "Introducing Ozzie United, captained by Ozzie

Ocala Holder." Again, she read off the names as Ozzie's team jogged onto the field in formation, chanting as they took up their positions. Two gym teachers stood in as linespersons, holding flags. "The referee of this match is our own Mr. Greenidge."

He ran onto the field dressed all in black carrying a new red-orange ball. He joined Ozzie and Victor in the centre ring. He presented each with a CAPTAIN's armband that they placed on their right arms. He showed a loonie to both of them.

"Tails," said Victor.

"Heads," said Ozzie.

Mr. Greenidge tossed the coin high in the air. The freshly minted brass colour glittered in the sunlight like gold. Ozzie was trying to recall the odds in favour of it being "heads" when it landed onto the short grass — as tails. Victor had won the kickoff.

The goalkeepers settled into position. Ozzie said his goalkeeper's oath, "I shall defend the gate to the castle with my life."

The referee placed the ball on the dot in the centre of the circle. He blew the opening whistle as loudly as if it was a World Cup final. Ozzie watched the game start:

Forward Muhammad slides the ball over to forward Sayid. Forward Ade and forward Sam move to cover them. Sayid sends the ball back to his midfielder Tarek who passes it over to midfielder Hassan.

The ball passed between them as they dribbled and looked for a way to get past Ozzie United. Four minutes had passed on Ozzie's stopwatch. This was turning into a boring match when...

Ade rushes and challenges Sayid, taking the ball away. Yes. Ozzie United gains possession for the first time. Ade signals to Sam. Sam is immediately covered by two midfielders. But instead of passing to Sam, Ade dribbles with lightning speed past the other two midfielders. Ezekiel, Sunny and Atah charge toward the Victor United defence. Ade draws two of their defenders to him. Before they reach him he quickly sends the ball high to Sam at the right side. Sam traps the ball on his chest. As it bounces to the ground he bends, looks for an opening, and kicks it hard with his left foot. With no defence to stop it, the ball zooms past Victor into the back of the net.

Goal! 1–0.

Sam extended his arms and glided like a bird. He was mobbed by his teammates, except for Ozzie and his defenders who held their positions, high-fiving each other. Ade was credited with the assist. Spectators cheered.

It worked, Ozzie thought. Tremendous speed and the element of surprise were their advantage.

For the next twelve minutes, Victor United kept possession of the ball most of the time. The goalkeepers saw little action. Forwards and midfielders from both teams did most of the battling. Ozzie continued calling the action in his head. He made mental notes for what he would say to his team during the break. He was so busy thinking that he did not hear Peter and Josiah calling to him. He snapped out of his 'state' as the ball hit the goal post to his right and dropped beyond the line behind him.

Goal! Equalizer. 1–1.

Muhammad, who had scored, performed two back flips. He started to take off his shirt until Sayid, nearby, waved his hands to stop him. Only in men's pro soccer was the removal of a shirt by a scorer in celebration permitted. If Sayid broke that rule, the referee could take the goal away.

Victor United celebrated. The spectators cheered the effort.

Ozzie wanted to kick himself.

"It's only one goal," Ade reassured him.

Ozzie regrouped quickly, putting it past him. *Every goalkeeper gets scored on some time*, he told himself.

Ozzie United kicked off the ball. But they were not able to do much with the last forty-five seconds in the half.

9
Keep Your Eyes on the Ball

Both teams grabbed bottles of water. Ozzie saw Mr. Greenidge talking to Principal Arsenault. So far, as ref, Mr. Greenidge had been fair, not favouring either team. No yellow cards. No red cards. Everyone was behaving.

Ozzie United sat at one end of the field. Ozzie made upbeat remarks. He praised his team's efforts and gave tips to players. They planned how to play the second half.

"Twenty minutes left, guys. A draw is not as exciting as someone winning. So let us knights be victorious for the kingdom. Also, when the ball crosses the side line and you win a throw-in, do it quickly. What else?" he asked.

"They always hog the ball," Sam complained.

"When they do that chase them, mark them, keep on them. They'll make mistakes. Use twice the speed when you need to. You can rest afterwards. You can sleep in tomorrow until noon. Tell your parents I, Ozzie Ocala Holder, give permission." He was fired up and his players caught his humour.

Keep Your Eyes on the Ball

In the second half, Kenneth replaced Atah as a forward. Each time Ozzie United had the ball they got past the forwards and midfielders. But Victor United's defence held them off. Ade and Sunny's separate shots on goal were waist high and caught easily by Victor. The spectators were vocal and loud, urging on both teams. Each time Victor United had possession of the ball Ozzie United was on them relentlessly.

Five minutes left in the match. Still 1–1. Sam marks midfielder Hassan. They are in our half. Our defenders are on the alert, shifting from side to side. Hassan slips into my penalty area, with Sam on his heels. He's really on his heels… Hassan stumbles forward to the ground as the ref blows his whistle and signals… No, it can't be. The ref signals a penalty kick. At the goal. At me.

Although Ozzie knew that Mr. Greenidge would be fair, he still turned to Peter.

"Did Sam push him?"

"Sure did," Peter replied. "What was he thinking?"

"Damn. I never said push. Never mind." Ozzie watched the ref place the ball on the penalty spot.

"Wall of Six!" Ozzie shouted.

Defenders Peter and Josiah stood on the outside of each goal post. Defender Owen, forward Ade and the four midfielders formed the wall, with Ozzie reminding them where to stand. Ozzie ran back to the goal line, looked, and shook his head.

"Ade, step out."

Ade stepped out completely, making it a Wall of Five.

Ozzie signalled to the ref that he was ready. The spectators started clapping in a slow rhythm.

Hassan takes two running steps. It looks like he will kick with his right foot... but he kicks with his left. The ball leaves the grass... Sure, we rehearsed that. The field was quiet then. Now, I can't hear myself think over the noisy crowd. I keep my eye on the ball. My Wall of Five covers their crown jewels. The ball lobs high over their heads, spinning. I can't tell if it is picking up speed or slowing down, heading right toward the centre of my goal. I am the last line of defence. I have to defend the castle. I have to protect the queen. I have seen this play many times. I spring from my right leg, arms straight up. If I am not high enough, the ball will sail over me and into the back of the net. I cannot lean back. I keep straight. The ball touches the tips of my gloves and I push it backwards. Up. Up. Up over the top of the crossbar.

Saved!

The ref blew the final whistle. He gestured for Ozzie and Victor to join him in the centre circle of the field.

"Penalty shootout. Principal Arsenault wants a winner," he said.

Ozzie and Victor looked at each other and shrugged.

"We'll use that one." Mr. Greenidge pointed to the goal on the south side of the field. "Less sun in your eyes. Ozzie, Victor, pick your first three shooters. Best after three wins."

Ozzie chose Ade, Owen and Sunny right away, in that order. Victor tapped Muhammad, Hassan and Sayid. Ozzie was nervous. He knew that everything came down to his skills, his ability to stop those shooters. He did not know the tactics of the shooters he was about to face. How well had they read his reactions during the match?

"Keep your focus. Keep your eyes on the ball," he mumbled to himself.

Muhammad faked to the left but sent the ball low to Ozzie's right. Ozzie dived too late.

Goal!

Don't beat yourself up, keep going, Ozzie told himself.

Ade scored first on Victor. But as Hassan got ready to shoot, Ozzie did not know how to read him. Would he go low like Muhammad? Would he go high again because the distance was shorter? Ozzie and Hassan eyed each other. They knew there had to be a winner. Hassan sent the ball to Ozzie's left side. His left leg was his shorter leg. Ozzie kept his eye on the ball, not on Hassan. He dived and caught the ball.

Owen missed on his turn. So did Sayid, by a finger. That left Sunny. If he scored, the match was theirs. If he missed, they picked more shooters and kept on.

Sunny was unpredictable and funny. He enjoyed soccer with recklessness. Ozzie watched him place the ball and squint at Victor like he could barely make him out in the goal. Ozzie felt like turning away. How could he watch? But he had to. He was his team's leader.

Ozzie watched every microsecond of the kick. A cannon shot from Sunny's shoe started low, but gained quick height past a stunned, helpless, Victor. The ball flew into the back corner of the net.

It was the World Cup.

Ozzie United fell into a heap, crushing Sunny — the hero. Ozzie waved to Dylan who gave him a thumbs-up sign. Then he jogged over to Victor who was sitting in front of his goal.

"Victor, you played well," said Ozzie.

"You think?"

"Seriously. Yes. The score wasn't 7–1."

Ozzie extended his hand. Victor took it, standing up.

"Congratulations, Ozzie. Your team won a good game."

Principal Arsenault made a short speech to the crowd. She thanked the players and the spectators, wished everyone a Happy Thanksgiving and dismissed the students for the weekend.

Ozzie United was mobbed — especially by the girls. They took abundant selfies.

"Well done, footballers," said Mr. Greenidge. All players had rehydrated and sat in the gym, as he had asked. "Ozzie and Victor, you are captains of the highest order. I am happy to have witnessed such a strong display of talent by both teams right to the end." Mr. Greenidge glowed. "If any of you go on to play for the national squad or the Olympic team I'm telling you here and now I want free tickets."

"I praise your commitment to this presentation match," he continued. "Plus your hard work at your practices over the past two weeks. Now I encourage you to use that dedication to be friends, no longer competitors. You have a common interest and you can learn more about soccer from each other. Next year some of you will end up in the same high school and continue with soccer. You might even be teammates."

Ozzie was a little surprised when Victor took the lead and offered his captain's armband to him. Ozzie returned the gesture.

"Are you sure, Ozzie? You could sell it on eBay," Sunny joked.

"I'm sure," he replied.

He was dripping in victorious sweat and he felt good.

10
Giving Thanks

Aunt Lisa had delivered two cedar-planked, whole salmons, as commanded. The dining-room table was laden with food. There was a platter of steamed kingfish slices. Plantain had been done the Nigerian and Trini way, pounded with a large wooden mortar and pestle by Ozzie. His arms still ached. Okras were steamed in palm oil. Bitter melon, also called cara-ilie, was a necessary side dish. Red kidney beans were plated beside pigeon peas and lima beans. Next were sweet potatoes, boiled green bananas, bright orange pumpkin and a large, mixed green salad. Tiny bowls of mango chutney, tamarind chutney, medium-hot pepper sauce and suicidal-hot pepper sauce were scattered around the table. There were large, rounded coconut bakes and homemade bread.

A large plastic tub on the floor was filled with pop and beer bobbing in watery ice. Palm juice (a drink in green bottles from Nigeria) was also cooling in the tub. Desserts were on a side table: pumpkin pie, strawberry-rhubarb pie and an oversized apple pie. Two jugs of fresh coconut water sat near ginger beer from ginger Ozzie had offered to grate because he loved the scent. Sitting in the freezer, guarded by Ozzie the sentry, were two large tubs of — Uncle Russell swore that he woke up early that morning to churn it by hand, like in the twentieth century 'back home' — COCONUT ICE CREAM.

Jazz on steel pan played throughout the house on the warm Thanksgiving Monday afternoon. Since Easter, and even at the Caribbean festival they still called "Caribana," Uncle Russell had promised to reveal the secret of his coconut ice cream to Ozzie. But every time Ozzie asked, he was always too young.

"You're thirteen yet?" Uncle Russell asked Ozzie, waving him over to his chair on the back porch.

Ozzie nodded.

"You're sure? 'Cause what I have to impart cannot be imparted to a minor."

Ozzie sipped from his glass of coconut water and nodded vigorously.

"I'll give you two keys now." Uncle Russell held up three fingers and gulped from his bottle of Carib. "One, almond milk." He lowered one finger. "Two..." He looked around and whispered into Ozzie's ear as he lowered the second finger.

Ozzie's eyes went wide. He looked at the last up-raised finger. He couldn't wait until he turned sixteen to hear what other trade secrets Uncle Russell would impart to him.

"If you write it down, put the paper in a vault, you hear me?" After another swig Uncle Russell continued, "You married yet? You have children?"

Ozzie almost fell out of his chair, laughing.

"If you ever have children, pass it on."

Mom tapped a spoon against her glass of ginger beer to summon everyone. They all held hands around the cramped dining area. Mom blessed the food and thanked everyone for being a part of their Thanksgiving.

Mr. Gupta, Dad's friend, was thankful to be employed again. Auntie Louise (actually Mom's great-aunt) was thankful to be free of arthritis pain today and for being almost ninety. Mom's cousin Daisy was thankful to have made it to Scarborough alive. She and her partner, Gloria, had ridden their bicycles all the way from their downtown condo.

It was Ozzie's turn. "I am thankful for you, Mom and Dad, bringing me and Rebecca into your lives, amen," he said.

Dad's gratitude was for his family, for opportunities to grow and for the family's new soccer star. Ozzie wondered if "opportunities to grow" referred to Mom. Maybe she had decided.

Mom got teary as she started her list. "I am also grateful for new opportunities," she continued. "I asked Felix, Rebecca and Ozzie not to say anything.

But standing among you all today..." And she broke the family secret. Ozzie thought Mom looked uncertain. And she even said that she could not make up her mind.

Dad took a loaf of homemade bread, broke off a small piece and passed it to Mom. She did the same, passing it to everyone to begin the meal. Everyone piled their plate with food and spread out to find a place to eat. Ozzie sat beside Uncle Russell, waiting for more secrets. Instead of talking, Uncle Russell attacked his plate with noisy glee.

Ozzie, Dad, Uncle Russell, Mr. Stephenson (one of Dad's widowed clients) and Mr. Gupta retired to the basement with their desserts. They were just in time for a European Cup playoff match of England versus Croatia. Ozzie filed away more soccer tips. He didn't know when he would ever play a full match again. He would have to apply the knowledge to six-a-side as long as the good weather held out.

Long after the guests left with full bellies and the house was tidied, Ozzie and Rebecca sat in their room.

"I feel better about us moving," she said, sipping a bottle of palm juice. "I'm ready."

"Not me."

"It's not about you, Ozzie. Dad would be making a sacrifice by travelling four days every week. Mom could have a good career."

"She has a good career now."

"She deserves the best one she can have. We're lucky to have Mom and Dad."

Ozzie was silent for a moment. Then, "You ever think about them, Sis?" *Them* was their birth parents.

"I do from time to time."

"I sometimes imagine that they show up, ring the bell and we open the door and..."

More silence.

"Ozzie, in less than a year you'll be in grade nine. Even if we stay in Scarborough you might end up in a different school from Dylan and Ade and your soccer buddies."

"I'm okay with that. But when it's my life that might be changing..."

"Nothing remains the same for everyone."

A while later Ozzie went to the kitchen for a glass of water. He found Dad sitting at the table sipping a mug of tea, lost in thought.

"Dad? Are you okay?"

"Your mom's wrestling with herself."

"About her decision?"

Dad nodded. "You know, I was leaning toward Hamilton because as you get older... as a teenager... Tell me, Ozzie, have you ever been stopped by the police? Just walking the area?"

Ozzie shook his head.

"I have. Many times. Even when I was a child. I thought if we moved to Hamilton you could escape that experience. But according to the news, you might face it there too." He sipped his tea and continued, "No matter what comes in your life, Ozzie, stand still and face everything with grace and the God-given power of your being."

"I will."

Dad kissed Ozzie on his head. "Good night, son."

"'Night, Dad."

Ozzie stayed in the kitchen, thinking about facing things he did not want to face. Then he went and got Mom. He led her into the basement where Dad kept a whole wall of books. He did not want anyone to hear what he needed to say. They sat on the sofa.

"Something bothering you, son?" Mom asked gently.

"I want you to know that I'm okay with whatever decision you make." Ozzie was surprised. It was easier to say than he thought it would be.

Mom looked at him and tears welled up in her eyes. She hugged him. "I'm so glad you said that."

"Me too, Mom."

And he meant it.

11
Present and Past

The school week started well. Ozzie enjoyed celebrity status on Tuesday. On Wednesday after school he continued an easy six-a-side with Ozzie United. The schedule would continue until the weather became too cold to play.

Thursday, after the main announcements, Ozzie and Victor were summoned to Principal Arsenault's office. They walked silently along the main hallway side by side. The school secretary directed them to the same chairs they had sat in two weeks before. The office door was closed.

"Did we have a fight or something that I don't remember?" asked Ozzie.

Victor shook his head.

"I mean, I could have beaten you up in class and Mrs. Yee reported it and I..."

"No, no, other way around. I always forget after I beat people up," Victor deadpanned.

"Right. You think we're being suspended for

something we did or something we didn't do?"

Before Victor could answer Mr. Greenidge opened the squeaky door. He ushered them in silently. Principal Arsenault sat regally in her big desk chair.

What, no breakfast again? Ozzie felt like saying.

"Ozzie and Victor, please sit," Mr. Greenidge said. How serious these adults looked!

"I'll get right to the point," said Principal Arsenault.

"Whatever it is we didn't do it," said Ozzie nervously.

"Yes, you did," Principal Arsenault raised her voice. Then she exchanged sly smiles with Mr. Greenidge. "You both held up your end of the bargain and entertained the school." *Bargain? I thought it was a royal command*, thought Ozzie.

"For doing so, both of you and your teammates will receive a reward. You will go with Mr. Greenidge to watch the Grade seven/eight soccer Division Championship next week at Birchmount Stadium."

Ozzie breathed a sigh of relief. He turned to Victor and, for the first time, they high-fived.

"Defending champs Agincourt Archers will be playing Kingston Bluffers," Mr. Greenidge added.

"Will we be going by jet?" Ozzie asked.

"Oh, yes. The jet is yellow, has six wheels and a horn," replied Principal Arsenault without missing a beat.

⚽ ⚽ ⚽

William Hall PS would celebrate Heritage Day on the third Tuesday of October. Ozzie spent his usual Saturday morning at Malvern Public Library after his chores. He was there to rewrite the story he had chosen for his assignment. He needed to put it into a rhythm. This was something new to him. Dad had promised to help on Sunday.

Earlier that morning Mom, Dad and Rebecca had left for Hamilton to check out the area. Mom had given the Hamilton hospital their answer — yes — the day before, and had given Scarborough Centenary Hospital one month's notice.

Ozzie stopped working around noon. Packing up his papers, he turned and saw Victor at the main desk. Victor was talking with a librarian. So it *had* been Victor he had seen before. Ozzie wondered what brought Victor to the library on Saturday mornings.

Instead of heading straight out past the main desk, Ozzie walked over to the adult fiction section. Pretending to browse, he walked backwards through the stacks... Atwood... Armstrong... Alexis... Achebe... *Things Fall Apart*. Here was a copy of the book, the only book he brought over from Nigeria. He opened it and flipped through the worn pages.

One day I'll finally read it, Ozzie thought as he closed it and put it back on the shelf. Then he noticed a sign: "Please Do Not Reshelve Library Materials, Survey in Progress." He took the book again and left it on a table. By the time he reached the main desk, Victor was gone. Good. Ozzie didn't feel like talking to him anyway.

Walking out of the library, Ozzie grabbed an apple out of his pack and bit into it. Across the way, he could see Dylan finishing his speed work on Blessed Mother Teresa school's track. Dylan and his cross-country team had qualified for the finals to be held the next Friday.

Ozzie looked around. He thought of Mom and Dad showing Rebecca her new high school — soon to be his new high school in the fall. Rebecca had been excited about visiting a mall five times bigger than Malvern Town Centre.

Ozzie knew that he would miss Malvern.

⚽ ⚽ ⚽

Ozzie stood in front of his class wearing a colourful African print shirt. It had a round neck and short sleeves, and was collarless. He waited until he had the class's full attention. Only then did he start to sing, without music, in the style of a Trinidad & Tobago calypso.

Mama Osun was a Nigerian goddess
She lived many years ago
Her beauty was like no other female
The ancestors told us so

Team Fugee

Mama Osun was a healer of sick
She watched over the lost and poor
Some say she appeared like a mermaid
A fresh water goddess from my folklore

Mama Osun brought teaching to humans
She wore yellow adorned with gold
Her husband was the god called Shango
She loved certain things we're told

Ozzie sang the chorus in upbeat Nigerian HighLife style:

She loves honey
She loves oranges
She loves pumpkin
She loves sweets
Honey, oranges, pumpkin, sweets
Honey, oranges, pumpkin, sweets
Honey, oranges, pumpkin, sweets

After more verses about Mama Osun, the Mother of Sweetness, he launched into the joyful chorus again. He drummed the desk in front of him and got his classmates to join in:

Present and Past

Honey, oranges, pumpkin, sweets
Honey, oranges, pumpkin, sweets
Honey, oranges, pumpkin, sweets

Mrs. Yee signalled that his time was up. He stopped short of having his classmates dance on their desks.

Next was Dylan who recited "Fern Hill," a poem by his namesake, Dylan Thomas, a Welsh poet. Dylan's voice was like music as he spoke of a childhood of wonder in a farm setting of nature, sun, moon and sky. Ozzie began to think that Dylan recited poems in his head while cross-country running.

The final presenter was Victor. He stood in front of the class and held up a small flag. He said, "Syria." Then he crossed to the door and switched off the front lights. On the SMART Board was a picture of beautiful mountains, a green hillside with wildflowers, a farmer with goats. The class saw a city street with outdoor cafes, happy faces, outside and inside of a huge mosque, children playing soccer on a street, a market with fresh and dried fruits, vegetables and other items. There was a big mall with an indoor roller-skating rink where children skated while adults sat at tables, beside a fountain, drinking coffee and eating pastries.

The screen went blank for a few seconds. Then it showed a soldier with a gun, buildings blown out by bombs, heaps of rubble, tanks, dead bodies in the street with limbs missing... blood.

Victor switched on the lights and returned to the centre saying,

"My household — mother, father, younger brother, grandfather and me. My uncle disappeared. He was a lawyer. My father paid money to find him, but we never knew anything. His wife (my aunt) and my three cousins were killed. That's when we knew we had to leave. We left Damascus and headed to Lebanon with very little. My grandfather died along the way and we buried him. We could not mark the grave."

Victor held up a small Canadian flag and continued. "My brother came to Canada with weak lungs. He's still getting better. We were the lucky ones. My grandfather..."

Ozzie could see that Victor was struggling not to cry. He thought of his own birth parents. Disappeared. And presumed dead.

"I miss him," Victor blurted out. And he cried. Mrs. Yee went over and put her arm around his shoulders.

Ozzie blinked back his own tears.

12
Field Trip

The yellow, six-wheeler bus chugged along Kingston Road, carrying the Ozzie United and Victor United teams. The players sat easily with each other, no longer rival teams. Ozzie sat in a window seat alone in the middle of the bus. He heard the drums of the marching band as Birchmount Stadium came into view.

"Look, cheerleaders!" Sunny shouted.

"In your dreams," replied Ade.

The bus turned right onto Birchmount Road, blocking the field.

"Actually, each school has their own marching band. And, yes, cheerleaders borrowed from the football teams only for today," said Mr. Greenidge.

Ozzie could see that the stadium was smaller than BMO Field stadium Dad had taken him to the year before. But it was impressive for a game between Grade seven/eight teams.

The Kingston Bluffers, challengers in navy blue, warmed up on the north half of the field. The Agincourt

Archers, defending champs in orange, occupied the southern half. Mr. Greenidge had told them that the stadium held two thousand, and it was full. The Grade seven/eight spectators included many Scarborough area schools with soccer programs that had competed for this championship. The other seats were taken by parents, coaches, school officials and the media. Vendors with drinks and snacks were everywhere.

Ozzie realized those students could have been his Scarborough teammates and competitors in Grade nine. He could have played on this field in the future. But instead he was moving to Hamilton.

Canada, even though I spoke English?

He settled into a seat beside Ade and Josiah. They were high above the green artificial turf with the sun to their backs.

Kickoff was at one-fifteen. The first half was uneventful. Defenders defended. Forwards and midfielders flowed up and down. The pace seemed slow, like the teams were trying to get to know each other, Ozzie figured. He was used to watching pro games with more excitement. He and Ade pointed out skillful attempts to each other. They laughed over flaws, like a Kingston Bluffer dribbling the ball and tripping over it. The match remained scoreless.

Whatever it was that the coaches said to their teams during the halftime break, it worked. They returned fired up. The defending champs drew first blood with a clean goal. The Kingston Bluffers, feeling the sting, reacted with a vengeance. They lobbed. They passed. They secured seven corner kicks. They headed balls. They assisted each other, even though one of their forwards missed a shot to a completely open net. Their star forward got two goals. Twenty-two minutes after that first goal Kingston Bluffers were leading 3–1. The Agincourt Archers goalkeeper could not hide his disappointment. He crumbled.

"Five minutes to go," Josiah said to Ozzie.

"The mark of true champs is to commit to scoring until the end," Ade said wisely.

"I've seen teams score three goals in the last five minutes," Ozzie added. "The team that's ahead can't get arrogant and sloppy."

They watched the Kingston Bluffers dilly-dally with the ball, confident of their victory. Ozzie was not impressed with that strategy. But even he could see that they had secured a victory. They were the new champs — clean and square.

After the trophy and medal presentation ended, Ozzie saw Mr. Greenidge chatting with both coaches. It seemed he knew the Kingston Bluffer's coach well for he kissed her on the cheek. On the ride back to school there was much analyzing and replaying of goals scored. Stepping off the bus, Mr. Greenidge asked Ozzie what he honestly thought of the match.

"We would have beaten them both," he replied.

⚽ ⚽ ⚽

The next morning Ozzie arrived early at school. He was waiting in the parking lot to catch Ms. Birbalsingh to talk about a weekend assignment he had missed when Mr. Greenidge pulled up. Ozzie recognized the sound of Beethoven's Fifth symphony on steel pan pounding through the open windows. He smiled at the thought that Mr. Greenidge got charged up for his day like that.

"Good morning, Mr. Greenidge."

"Morning, Ozzie," he replied, exiting the suddenly silent car. "I've been thinking about what you said yesterday. If I can arrange an exhibition match with the Kingston Bluffers, would you be interested?"

"You're teasing, right?"

Could Ozzie United take the field again?

"I never tease... on Fridays. I'll get back to you," he said, walking off. "Not a word to anyone."

That afternoon Ozzie watched as Dylan placed fourth at his cross-country finals. Overall, the William Hall PS Grade seven/eight team placed fifth. Each member had posted a personal best. Ozzie had a new appreciation of Dylan's athletic commitment. He was aware of how hard Dylan had trained. He knew that he too would have to work harder and commit to becoming a better goalkeeper.

13
Out of the Comfort Zone

At the beginning of lunchtime on Monday, Mr. Greenidge caught Ozzie before he reached his locker. They walked along the hallway away from his friends.

"Ozzie, I have good news and I have good news," said Mr. Greenidge. "Which do you want to hear first?"

"The first good news first." Ozzie smiled.

"The Kingston Bluffers have agreed to a friendly match next week."

"No way."

"Yes, way."

"All right! You are the best, Mr. G!" Ozzie exclaimed. "And the second good news?"

"The match cannot be against Ozzie United only. Victor's team needs to play too."

"But that's not good news. We won."

"Yes."

"It's not fair."

"That's why I'm meeting with you before anyone else."

Ozzie didn't know what to say.

"See how this fits for you," continued Mr. Greenidge. "There's a bigger picture here, Ozzie. A mixture of players from both teams will give a better representation of William Hall."

Ozzie was silent. He didn't like it, but he took it in.

"I'd like you to take the rest of your lunch period to think this over, Ozzie. If you don't want to do it, I'll cancel the whole thing, no problem. Let me know."

Ozzie left his lunch in his locker and strolled over to Malvern Town Centre, entering near the No Frills supermarket. He did not want to run into his team and have to ask their opinion.

He avoided the food court and walked past the kiosk that played reggae. Usually he would chat with the owner about calypso, soca and chutney music. But he stopped when he saw Principal Arsenault coming out of a gift shop, carrying a large bag.

"Ozzie, why are you looking so glum?" she asked.

He figured that she already knew. Mr. Greenidge had to have received her permission.

"Mr. Greenidge…"

"So you've had a talk. I'm curious, are you worried about the match? It's an exhibition."

"*My team* should be playing the Kingston Bluffers."

She led him over to a bench where they sat down. "You are right. When I was principal at a school on the Six Nations of the Grand River Reserve..."

Ozzie recalled that the Grand River was in Brantford, way past Hamilton.

"... I got a call asking me if I would head up William Hall PS. I said no."

"Why?"

"I was raised on the reserve. When I went to McMaster University in Hamilton on a basketball scholarship, I mixed with people from all over the world, returned to the reserve as a teacher and then principal. I was comfortable among my people. When the call about William Hall came again, I met with an elder. She advised me to get out of my comfort zone and grow. She said the change would be good for me. Here I am."

There was that word again, "change," Ozzie thought.

Ozzie stared at the gift bag Principal Arsenault was holding. She took out the item and unwrapped it. It was a large round piece of stained glass. She held it up to the light. Two white owls with green eyes, side by side, stared out at Ozzie.

"Neat."

"Snowy owls. My grandparents' wedding anniversary is this weekend. They have great intuition, my grandparents."

She repacked it, looked at her watch and stood up. "Ozzie, when in the past did you have to work with new people?"

"It was when I organized six-a-side. Even though we all came from Nigeria as refugees we came from different parts. We didn't arrive in Canada at the same time. Some of us were adopted by Canadian parents, and some came with their families."

"Yet you managed to bring them all together as a team," she said. "I really admire that kind of leadership."

"I think I'll talk to Mr. Greenidge again," said Ozzie slowly.

"You can only grow from the experience."

He nodded.

"Need a ride back?"

"That wouldn't be cool."

"Okay. I get it. See you."

"Bye, Principal Arsenault."

When she was out of sight Ozzie ran past the music kiosk, which was playing a soca he did not recognize. He dashed past the food court and out of the centre. He rushed across the west parking lot to the school's staff room. Breathlessly, he asked a teacher going in the door if she would find out if Mr. Greenidge was there. Seconds later Mr. Greenidge came out, chewing his lunch. He had a piece of what looked like spinach stuck to his teeth.

"I'm ready to talk, Mr. Greenidge," Ozzie blurted out.

Several minutes later they met with Victor in the Ozzie United Room. Mr. Greenidge explained to

Victor about the friendly match.

"So you each pick five players," Mr. Greenidge said.

"I want Dylan Hollingsworth on the team," said Ozzie boldly.

"Not a chance," Victor objected. "He can't be one of us. He's a cross-country runner."

"Dylan's played with us many times. He's in good condition. And he would be a strong midfielder," Ozzie argued.

"How come he only placed fourth?"

"Fourth is pretty good. Have you ever run a race?" Ozzie challenged.

"Okay, guys," Mr. Greenidge interrupted.

"I'm not giving up any players," Victor said with finality, crossing his arms.

"Fine. I will," Ozzie offered.

"Deal," Victor said quickly before Ozzie changed his mind.

"Give me your first choices and positions right now," Mr. Greenidge said, moving to the board with a marker. "There will be four substitutes. Two each."

He wrote as they offered their choices.

"Some guys won't be happy," Ozzie said.

"I'll take care of that," Mr. Greenidge assured them. "It will be okay."

"I hope you are right," said Victor.

The buzzer announced that lunch period was over. Ozzie had forgotten to eat.

"Gather everyone and we'll meet in the gym after school," Mr. Greenidge said.

Ozzie knew that he had one more thing to say.

"Mr. Greenidge, there's a piece of salad on your tooth."

14
Hall United

A new team named HALL UNITED was made. This team had six Syrians, five Nigerians and a Welsh boy. There were two Syrian and two Nigerian substitutes, and nine coaching assistants, for a total of twenty-five players.

Mr. Greenidge handed out the list of positions and duties and the practice schedule. There was much chatter and grumbling. He clapped his hands to get their attention.

"Good afternoon, footballers. William Hall has been given a unique opportunity. As you can see, everyone will be involved. Those of you not playing on the field will be my assistants and trainers. I take full responsibility for selecting you and assigning posts and positions, as a one-time coach for this exhibition."

Ozzie was relieved that Mr. Greenidge had taken any heat off him and Victor.

"Principal Arsenault and I hope that a showcase of your collective, and I mean collective, talents will pave the way for this school to have a full soccer program for both boys and girls," he continued.

"When will that be, Coach?" Sunny asked.

"Possibly next year. We're not sure," he replied. "I know most of you will be in high school by then. Those in Grade seven will benefit directly."

"I'm in Grade seven," Peter spoke up. "If we get beaten 20–0 by the champs, how will that benefit us?"

"Yeah, we only have one week. It is impossible to win," said Hassan.

"We're gonna be slaughtered like turkeys at Thanksgiving," said Sunny.

Coach Greenidge held up a hand. "If that is your attitude this can end right here, right now," he said firmly and calmly. "You are not marching into a war as untrained soldiers, risking your young lives. This is a soccer match for those who will come after you." His voice began to rise. "You are brave giants upon whose shoulders others will one day stand. Not everything is about winning. Your co-captains, Ozzie and Victor, and I do not believe the score will be 20–0. Whatever it is, you will not be embarrassed. You will hold your heads up high. Am I right or am I right?"

Silence.

"I said, am I right or am I right?" he barked.

"Right, Coach!" they yelled in unison.

Tuesday morning the air was cool. Fall was beginning to show its presence. Early morning dew sparkled on the grass when Hall United started their first practice.

As planned with Ozzie and Victor, Coach Greenidge led them through drills and activities, without a big speech before or after. The lunch break would be for talks between Coach Greenidge and the co-captains or between the co-captains alone, as needed. The touch football team had been eliminated from the playoffs, so the field was also free after school.

The afternoon was a repeat of the morning's session. This time Coach Greenidge wanted to see how everyone cooperated. At the end, Coach Greenidge brought them into a circle, assistants included.

"Footballers, good sessions." He looked around at each and every one of them. "If I had a season to work with you, I'd coach you differently. With one week, I'm going to point out what you do well individually and how to improve that. I'll correct only what is necessary as we go along. In soccer, communication is key to playing as a team. Apart from silent signals that we work out between ourselves, English will be the only language spoken. You are a team. Act like one. No Syrian clique. No Nigerian clique. And definitely no Welsh clique." He pointed at Dylan, to chuckles among the boys.

Ozzie went to bed early, exhausted. He knew that he would have to pace himself through the week. At the next morning's practice, two assistants, Trevor and Sayid, shot penalty kicks to Ozzie and Victor in goal. On the rest of the field, Coach Greenidge had the new forwards and midfielders dribble the ball and pass to each other. Off to the side, two assistants, Kenneth and Yusuf, worked with the new defenders.

One morning, Principal Arsenault announced that anyone interested in soccer and who wanted to support Hall United should sign up with Coach Greenidge. There would be a school bus booked to take them to the friendly match.

At lunch on Thursday, Ozzie met with Coach Greenidge in the former Ozzie United room, now the Hall United room. They sat eating their lunches.

"Dylan told me that he stood in as referee for your six-a-side match before the presentation match. How was that?"

"Fine. He knows the game very well. That's why I trusted him to do that. Otherwise, it would have been a disaster."

"I've been thinking about a rehearsal match this Saturday afternoon. The new squad versus the rest."

Ozzie chewed, thinking over what he had heard.

"A match is a good idea. But, but, but... if the rest beat us what happens? Will they demand to be the new Hall United? Headline in the newspaper: WAR ERUPTS AT WILLIAM HALL PS."

"My coaching career would be over."

"Definitely."

"Right. Next idea."

"We could work on a couple of tactics on Saturday."

Hall United

"Do you have anything in mind?"

"The Double Cross. First a player has to win a corner kick. Most players, including the opposition will bunch up in front of the goal area. But one player will drift to the far side. Hopefully no one notices him. The kicker sends the ball, not to the centre area, but to the far side where the solo player waits for it. It will look like a bad cross to the opposition. But, and here's the tricky part, the solo player has to get the ball and send it to the middle quickly to someone who can shoot to goal."

"Now, *that is mas'!* We'll give it a try!" Coach Greenidge was jumping up and down.

15
Opposition

At supper Mom told Ozzie and Dad about a counteroffer she had received from Scarborough Centenary Hospital. Her boss, the Head of Paediatrics, would be retiring in December. The position was hers if she wanted it.

"I will have to let the hospital board know by next Friday," she said. "That's the day I have to confirm my acceptance of the Hamilton offer, too."

Two days after our match, Ozzie figured.

Staying would be great. But Ozzie was getting used to the idea of leaving Malvern and everything he knew. What if he went somewhere like Principal Arsenault did? Would he grow more if he went out of his comfort zone? What about the changes that had already happened? He was not only playing soccer, but he was leading his second team. He was confused.

Ozzie simply said to Mom, "You'll know what's best, Mom."

He had a friendly match to focus on.

Halloween was on Saturday. William Hall PS was

celebrating it on Friday. Knowing that he could not show up without a costume, Ozzie had told Mom and Dad to pick anything. That morning, in the living room was a Star Wars Jedi Knight costume, complete with lightsaber and a white tunic with brown, hooded robe.

Then he noticed Rebecca's black jumpsuit and platinum wig. She was Storm from Marvel's X-Men. *Dad said Storm was based on Oye, Nigerian goddess of storms and tornadoes,* Ozzie thought. *Rebecca can be stormy at times.*

Hall United had a light practice on the frosty morning. The team took turns shooting at Ozzie and Victor. Just before class, Ozzie put his costume on over his regular clothes in the change room.

"You won't guess. I'll tell you," said Dylan when Ozzie eyed his costume. "A Hobbit from Middle Wales. I wanted to come as Gollum. But I didn't want to spend the whole day almost naked."

"One way to get a girlfriend," Ozzie offered. He looked up as Victor joined them. "I don't get it, Victor."

"My parents said Aladdin or Arabian Prince — choose."

"Glasses. Black, mock turtleneck jersey. Black pants. Mock Apple tablet," said Dylan. "You chose Steve Jobs. Because of his Syrian heritage."

"A hero. I get it," Ozzie exclaimed.

"You knew that about Steve Jobs?" Victor asked Dylan.

"My dad would disagree, but I know everything," Dylan said.

Hiding behind his Jedi Knight mask, Ozzie overheard three students talking later that day.

"Taking on the Kingston Bluffers, how dumb is that, eh?" said Student A.

"Who do they think they are, Montreal Impact?" asked Student B.

"They think they're Manchester United, mate, in the bloody Barclays Premier League," said Student C in a mocking English accent.

"They're Leicester City, man, risen from the dead to become champions," Student A commented.

"Those Bluffers will kick them over the Scarborough bluffs, they will," Student C guffawed.

At least they know soccer teams, Ozzie mused.

"And what could that Welsh idiot, what's-his-name..." Student B asked.

"... Dylan," Student A replied.

"Yeah, Dylan. What's he doing with a bunch of Nigerians and Syrians?" Student B continued.

"Oh, didn't you know, he's a refugee. From the Co-op. Or is it the coop?" Student C snickered.

"None of them should be representing this school, if you ask me," Student B stated.

Ozzie kept quiet. This was not a moment to stand up and face anyone who thought like that.

After school Coach Greenidge reported that so

many students, both boys and girls, had already signed up for a ride to the game that he might have to order a second bus.

Ozzie introduced the surprise speed tactic which had frustrated Victor United. Coach Greenidge called a practice for the next day from two to four p.m.

"I did not put this on this schedule. If you cannot make it because of family commitments, that's okay. I'll work with whoever shows up. No pressure, guys. There's still Monday and Tuesday," he concluded.

Ozzie, Victor and Dylan made a pact with one another. They would be there.

Friday night the Holder household was almost empty. Rebecca was out with her friends. Mom and Dad were out with Mr. Gupta, to discuss Mom's dilemma, Ozzie presumed. He and Dylan relaxed by watching a Kevin Hart comedy. Ozzie wanted to mention what he had overheard the students say in the hallway. Could they be right? Was Hall United really playing out of their league? He decided not to bring up what Dad would call 'negativity.' Laughter was a good way to keep fears at bay.

⚽ ⚽ ⚽

Ozzie completed all of his weekend assignments at the library by noon on Saturday. He saw Victor coming out of the meeting room and waved to him. Victor approached him sheepishly.

"I take extra ESL class. I must better my English," he confessed.

"You don't have to be shy about that, Victor." He wanted to say "embarrassed" but "shy" was better. No need to make Victor feel bad.

"I want to stop others teasing me... when I... stumble with English."

Ozzie recalled his comment about Victor not reading that set off their fight in September. "I understand," he said, as he finally did.

"My secret. I share with you. Where did you learn to speak so good?"

"Nigeria. At an orphanage."

Ozzie realized how lucky he had been not to have language as a challenge when he got to Canada. He took Victor to the audio section and suggested some CDs for him to check out. They exited the main doors together. As they walked along Sewells Road, three older teens blocked their path on the sidewalk.

"Trick or treat, what are you two dressed as?" Teen #1 asked.

"I think they're dressed as fugees... *ref*-fugees." Teen #2 said.

Ozzie and Victor moved to the side but were blocked again.

"Why you two dressed up in nice Canadian costumes? You got suicide bombs under those costumes?" Teen #3 demanded.

Opposition

Ozzie was confused. *I'm not even Muslim.*

"I know, I know, you're from Serious. No, wait, Syria?" Teen #2 snickered.

Victor was about to speak. Ozzie stopped him.

"Three against two," Ozzie said in his boldest voice. "You're bigger, taller and stronger. The question you need to ask yourselves is, are you faster than a Grade eighter?" Before the words left his mouth, Ozzie grabbed Victor and pulled him away. They ran across the road, causing a car's tires to screech.

The teens chased them. But Ozzie and Victor ran with lightning speed, backpacks on their backs, across Neilson toward the busy east side parking lot of Malvern Town Centre. When he dared a look behind them, Ozzie realized that the teens had given up. Besides, there were too many witnesses. Ozzie and Victor stopped, panting and laughing together.

"Will I always be seen as refugee?" Victor asked.

"You can't think about that."

"What to do then? Run away?"

"With some guys you stand up and face them. With others you leave their presence. Even my Dad still faces situations and he was born here. Don't let them steal your joy, that's all."

"I'll remember that," Victor said. "See you at the practice, Ozzie."

"Later," replied Ozzie.

16
Coming Together

Two hours later all Hall United players gathered at the school's field. Four of the nine assistants showed up as well. It was a light practice involving a step by step breakdown of movements. Since it was outside of a school day, no one was covered by insurance. Coach Greenidge could not risk injuries, so no actual play.

Mr. Greenidge patiently explained the Four-Step Poker Dance, moving three players around to show them the plan. "A passes sideways to B who passes ahead to C. Meanwhile A runs ahead to be in line with C. C passes to A who shoots to the goal. If executed properly it will be ten times faster than it sounds."

"What about their defence?"

"You cannot give the Bluffers a chance to see what you are doing," Coach Greenidge said. "If you manage to do it once in a match, you won't get a second chance. You are playing the Bluffers, yes, but you would be bluffing them."

"Let's call it Bluff the Bluffers, then," offered Sunny.

"What if they hear you?" asked Victor. "It would be game done."

I'm sure he meant 'game over,' thought Ozzie. He said, "If we call out Four-Step Poker Dance only we will know what that means."

"Okay. Once more," Coach Greenidge said.

Once more became eight times more. Then Coach Greenidge handed out bottled juices, water and oranges. After the break, Ozzie and Victor positioned the forwards and midfielders. Ozzie placed the four substitutes as Bluffers in front of the goal area.

"What we are going to teach you is called the Double Cross," Ozzie said.

⚽ ⚽ ⚽

Ozzie and Dylan walked together afterwards.

"My Dad wanted to buy me new gloves," said Ozzie. "I said no. There's not enough time to break them in properly."

"Ozzie, you're lucky to have your Dad support you like that. My Dad thinks I should have won cross-country. If he knew I was playing soccer he'd be laughing his head off," Dylan said, shaking his head sadly. "He'd say, 'Bring me the man who put you up to this nonsense. I want to look into his eyes.'"

"Poor Coach Greenidge, facing your father. No,

you'd have to send him Principal Arsenault instead."

"She's almost twice my dad's height. He'd have to stand on a barrel to challenge her, he would," Dylan said.

That image cracked them up.

"Sure you don't want to go trick or treating later?" Dylan asked.

"Positive. Yesterday was enough for me. Besides, I'm getting too old for that."

"Hmm. Text me if you change your mind."

They bumped fists and went their separate ways. One thing Ozzie knew for certain: The team was coming together. How well they would do next Wednesday was left to be seen.

⚽ ⚽ ⚽

Ozzie was the first to arrive at the Monday practice. November had brought fall in full colourful splendour. A year ago most of the leaves were already on the ground by this time. Some people said it was global warming. Some said it was global cooling. Ozzie hadn't decided who was right. He was glad to be wearing gloves and feeling well rested after two nights of ten-hour sleeps.

The drills included the Four-Step Poker Dance and the Double Cross and other tactics. Coach Greenidge stated that Victor would be the first-half goalkeeper and Ozzie would play the second half.

Principal Arsenault announced that the character

word for November was *Compassion*.

At lunchtime Victor invited Ozzie to walk over to Malvern Town Centre. He told him to leave his lunch in his locker. Ozzie was curious but did as asked. They arrived at the newly opened stall in the food court, Falafel of the Desert. Victor treated Ozzie to a tahini-dripping falafel and raspberry juice.

"This is so good, Victor," Ozzie said, taking a huge bite of his wrapped sandwich. "Thanks."

"I am happy you enjoy it. Yesterday I listened to one of the CDs you showed me at the library. I played back and spoke aloud. It's good. Thank you."

"Anytime," Ozzie mumbled around the food in his mouth. He wondered if he would find falafels in Hamilton.

Victor went back to Falafel of the Desert and brought two wax-paper-wrapped items to the table. He handed one to Ozzie.

"What's in the pastry?" Ozzie asked, peeling the paper from the treat.

"Pistachios. Walnuts. A light sugar syrup. Ancient Syrian spices," Victor replied. Through a sweet sticky mouthful, he asked Ozzie, "What you think of Coach Greenidge?"

"I like him. No other gym teacher wanted to restart a soccer program here."

"You think we are like lamb?"

"What do you mean?"

"Lambs get killed to make *shawarma*."

"I don't care. I'm getting to play soccer. And I'm glad we're playing together."

"Me too," Victor said, smiling. "You know, Mr. Greenidge wants to be super coach. That's okay."

As they walked back to school Victor pointed at Lester B. Pearson Collegiate Institute.

"I'm going there next year. What about you?"

That caught Ozzie off guard. "I... I haven't decided yet."

"They have a good soccer program. Maybe we will play together."

"Maybe," Ozzie replied. He was not about to say that he'd probably be in Hamilton. But he thought that it was beginning to look that way — a brand new hospital; a bigger house. Ozzie would be forced out of his comfort zone. He figured if they were staying in Malvern, Mom would have decided already. Friday was four days away. "Thanks for lunch, Victor," was all he said.

"You are, as they say, quite welcome." Victor smiled.

⚽ ⚽ ⚽

During afternoon practice Ozzie was distracted. He could not focus and he wondered why.

At home, it all came crashing down on him in the basement. His breath became short.

Maybe those guys were right.

Coming Together

Who did we think we were, going up against the champion Kingston Bluffers?

A bunch of refugees. Fugees.

Why did I boast to Coach Greenidge?

Why is Mom making us move to Hamilton?

His chest felt tight. He called out to Rebecca who was upstairs in the kitchen, warming up supper. She came rushing down.

Ozzie told his sister everything that was on his mind. She held him as he sobbed. They had to play the memory game for a long time before Ozzie felt better.

17
A Friendly Match

Today was going to be the biggest match of Ozzie's life — so far. He awoke rested and calm. He stood in the shower, wondering if he would have another attack of nerves. After dressing, he removed his beaded chain and placed it on his dresser.

Ozzie moved through his morning classes in a daze. After lunch Hall United changed into their uniforms: red T-shirts with the school crest over their hearts and HALL UNITED silk-screened on their backs. The players and assistants crammed into the Hall United Room. They had one last thing to rehearse — their chant and procession.

As they finished, Principal Arsenault knocked and entered. She looked up at the cobwebbed ceiling and the filthy floor beneath her before settling her gaze on everyone.

"Good morning, Hall United."

"Good morning, Principal Arsenault," they replied almost together.

A Friendly Match

"I want to say that I appreciate all of you putting your talents on display for a good cause. Have an enjoyable match."

Ozzie felt the bus ride along Kingston Road was different this time. Instead of going to watch, they were a soccer team. Instead of one lone school bus, there were three: one for Hall United and two carrying about one hundred William Hall PS supporters.

Sitting beside Dylan, Ozzie began to get nervous. He closed his eyes to relax, playing memory game alone. He found a good-feeling place as the images drifted from Nigeria to Canada:

The family dancing to steel pan music on Caribana Day.

Tobogganing with Dylan in Rouge Park and tumbling in the snow.

Dad belly-flopping in the pool at Toronto Pan Am Sports Centre.

He opened his eyes before the bus turned onto Birchmount Road. No school band. No visible cheerleaders. But the Kingston Bluffers did have a large crowd.

As the Kingston Bluffers fans sang their school song and shouted the chant Ozzie remembered from almost two weeks ago, he suddenly saw Birchmount Stadium as a Roman coliseum. The crowd was made up of citizens foaming at the mouth for blood, Hall United's blood, his blood. The players of Hall United were not real gladiators in their eyes. They were upstarts. Principal Arsenault sat beside the Emperor, Superintendent Dominski. She had offered them up as entertainment. The ball was not a soccer ball. It was Ozzie's head.

Ozzie shook the images from his head.

After the teams had warmed up, Superintendent Dominski welcomed the crowd. As guests, Hall United was introduced first. To a mixture of cheers from their fans and polite applause from Bluffers fans, they chanted:

We're Hall United
We're high spirited
United we stand
United we succeed
Hall United, Hall United

They repeated the chant, gaining vocal strength and confidence as each player took his position on the field. Victor settled in the centre circle with the referee. Ozzie took a position in line with the midfielders.

As Superintendent Dominski introduced the Kingston Bluffers, they ran onto the field and took their positions. They were all business, no chants. It was their supporters who chanted.

The Bluffers won the coin toss and led the kickoff. Taking possession of the ball, they seemed to be toying with Hall United. They kept the ball in their half.

They dared forwards Ade, Muhammad and Sam to take the ball away. Ozzie, along with midfielders Hassan, Tarek and Sunny, followed them. Yet Ozzie had seen this tactic before against Agincourt Archers."Hassan, Sunny, fall back, now!" he yelled.

They looked at him with confusion.

"*Now*, guys!" he yelled as he saw the Bluffers forwards break away. Hassan and Sunny joined him, jogging backwards. A Bluffers defender rolled the ball to their goalkeeper, who kicked it high past the centre line to where Ozzie, Hassan and Sunny had fallen back. Meanwhile, the Bluffers forwards had bounded toward the area, hoping to get the expected ball. Hassan trapped it and lobbed it back over the centre line toward Muhammad, who headed it over to Sam. But neither team could score.

By the time Coach Greenidge called for substitution, Ozzie had touched the ball with his feet only a few times. He trotted off, exaggerating his limp. The laughter from the opposition did not faze him. There was a plan. At the side line he slapped both palms with Dylan.

"Show no mercy," he said to Dylan.

In that moment he thought of the character word for November, *Compassion*.

"Screw that, compassion can come later. This is soccer," Ozzie whispered to himself.

Coach Greenidge greeted him with a knocked fist. "Good, man."

"I hope this works," Ozzie said.

"They have tactics. We have tactics. I think they underestimate your abilities," Coach Greenidge said confidently.

Ozzie took up a spot behind the sideline near Victor with a full view of the entire field. Less than a minute after play resumed, Sam stole the ball. Ozzie started the play-by-play in his head:

Sam dribbles the ball across the centre line. He passes it to Hassan who passes it back to Sam. Sam looks ahead toward the Bluffers goal area and sees Tarek and Sunny near the Bluffers defenders. He lobs it high. Tarek, Sunny and the defenders all jump. Sunny's head connects with the ball first, directing it to the right. The Bluffers goalkeeper dives in the wrong direction. Well, wrong direction for him. The ball floats into the back right corner of the net — where it rightfully belongs.

Brilliant Goal! 1–0.

Sunny ran toward the area where Hall United spectators were cheering wildly. He fell to his knees and raised his hands high. Teammates mobbed him in celebration. Ozzie and Coach Greenidge bumped fists. Hall United had drawn first blood.

"Keep alert, Victor!" Ozzie shouted to the goalkeeper.

Victor gave a thumbs-up.

Both teams repositioned. Kingston Bluffers kicked off. True to form, they began an aggressive attack as if to say no more toying with these upstarts.

A Friendly Match

Bluffers forwards charge. Their star player scissor-kicks the ball toward Victor who catches it easily, hugging it to his chest. Victor throws the ball to defender Owen who passes it to Dylan who passes to Tarek. The ball is stolen from Tarek by a Bluffers midfielder. The Bluffers begin another charge toward a congested area in front of Victor. The ball is toed high. A Bluffers forward heads the ball, but not to the goal as Victor expects. He heads it softly over to his teammate, who heads it to the Bluffers star forward on his left. The forward heads it into the corner of the net.

Outstanding Goal! 1–1.

The Bluffers star forward front-flipped and landed on both feet like a gymnast. His teammates covered him as they celebrated, while their spectators cheered like they had won the match. But still they wanted more blood, Hall United's blood.

"That's a tripleheader, very rare. Victor could not have known," Coach Greenidge said to Ozzie.

"Tricky," said Ozzie. "What else have they got planned for us?"

Ozzie cupped his mouth with his hands and shouted, "Victor. Recover quickly. It's one goal. You'll have more chances to save!"

Victor again gave a thumbs-up and forced a slight smile.

Ozzie was right. The Bluffers continued their dominant attacks. Victor saved three more shots on goal. Hall United's supporters chanted:

Hall United
Da da / da da / da da
We want a goal
Da da / da da / da da

With four minutes before halftime, Coach Greenidge signalled for the four substitutes to start warming up. He shaped an 'X' in front of his body with his fingers. Tarek was the first to notice. Soon he was passing the signal along to Hall United's forwards and midfielders.

Hassan chases the ball against a Bluffers defender. They jostle straight to the left of the Bluffers goalkeeper. The ball crosses the line off the defender to award Hassan the corner. Most of the players gather in front of the goal area. Dylan drifts toward the opposite corner, unchecked. Hassan blows out a breath. Coach Greenidge seems to be holding his breath. Hassan settles the ball in the corner arc and steps back. Without giving away what he plans to do, he crouches and steps forward, toeing the ball high over everyone's head. The Bluffers chuckle as if it is the worst move they have ever seen. But Dylan traps the ball and instantly kicks it centre to an opening. Muhammad stops the ball enough to control its spin. Then he aims it into the net's left corner with such speed that the keeper has no time to block it.

Lightning Goal! 2–1.

The Kingston Bluffers spectators went silent. The smaller group of Hall United supporters made the noise of ten thousand. Muhammad was mobbed by his teammates. Ozzie and Coach Greenidge, who was breathing again, bumped fists.

Bam. Bam. Bam.

Hassan, Dylan and Muhammad were not playing in the same combination as when they had trained for Double Cross at practice. They must have paid attention well. Ozzie marvelled at the poetry of it. He and Victor exchanged a thumbs-up, smiling. With one minute left on the clock, Ozzie started his warm-up.

18
An Act of Compassion

"The Kingston Bluffers are a strong comeback squad," Coach Greenidge said during halftime while everyone sipped water. "Their coach, Ms. Jeong-Hough, played in the World Cup for South Korea. She knows tactics. Don't assume because you're leading by a goal that the match is won. Find chances to score."

Ozzie was now dressed as a white-shirted goalkeeper with the CAPTAIN's armband on. He shared what he had observed from the sideline. Victor told Ozzie which strikers to watch out for.

Ozzie settled into goal and said his private oath: "I shall defend the gate to the castle with my life."

From the beginning of the second half, the Bluffers seemed bent on winning. One of their midfielders received a yellow card for tripping Ade. Sure, it was an exhibition, but rules were rules. Ade's penalty kick bounced off the Bluffers Wall of Six. Ozzie wished the kick had been a little higher to give Ade a good chance to score.

An Act of Compassion

From his goal, Ozzie began to see a constant changeover of the ball. Back and forth it went between players on the same team and between teams.

Change. There it was. Small change. Big change. What was in that word I feared? Ozzie thought. *Hamilton. Scarborough. I would still be with Rebecca, Mom, Dad…*

Suddenly a Bluffers striker ran toward the penalty box area. He received the ball and curled it in toward the goal. Ozzie snapped out of his trance and dived — in the wrong direction.

Exquisite Goal! 2–2.

In the microsecond before celebrations broke out in the Bluffers stands a whistle was blown. But for whom? The Bluffers looked to their coach. She shrugged her shoulders. The striker was ruled offside. No goal allowed.

From the sideline Victor shouted, "Keep your focus, Ozzie! You're doing okay!"

Ozzie knew he had to do better than okay. He could not let the squad down. He clearly saw the next shot on his goal. Instead of waiting for the ball, he stepped toward it, jumped and caught it. He quickly bowled it over to Riad.

Hall United supporters chanted, repeating:

Hall United, Hall United
Give us another goal
Hall United, Hall United
You are worth your weight in gold

Hall United midfielders charged forward but lost the ball before they crossed the centre line. A Bluffers midfielder gained the corner to Ozzie's right. Ozzie saw the star striker and another striker taking up positions within his penalty box. The midfielder aimed and missed the ball completely. Trying again, he kicked high toward a forward. Instead of heading it toward Ozzie's goal, the forward headed it over to the star striker, who wasted no time heading it toward Ozzie. Ozzie held his position and caught it as it slammed into his chest. Had he fallen backwards it would have been a goal. But the doubleheader did not work a second time. Ozzie drop-kicked the ball away.

I swore an oath to defend the castle with my life. But this hurts, he thought.

Desperation crept onto the faces of the Kingston Bluffers. Ozzie clapped his gloves together rapidly. It was a signal. With fifteen minutes left on the clock Hall United went into high gear. *Surprise Speed*. Hall United, united silently in mind, was not going to allow Kingston Bluffers any more chances.

Dylan fired a scissor kick. It was a missile. Ozzie, from his goal must have blinked. All he saw was the ball dropping to the ground at the back of the net. And then the team mobbing Dylan.

Spectacular Goal! 3–1.

Two minutes later, Muhammad stole the ball from the Bluffers striker. Several players from both teams bunched in front of the Bluffers goalkeeper. Ade had his back to the goal. When Peter slipped the ball to him, Ade stopped it with the sole of his shoe and kicked it directly backwards with his heel. He did not even look behind him. The reaction of his teammates told the story. Once again, Ozzie did not see it. The celebration said everything.

Delightful Goal! 4-1.

Four minutes left. Ozzie shouted to his defenders. "No mercy!"

Coach Greenidge gave them a signal.

Ozzie could hear his teammates saying four words. Time to run the Four-Step Poker Dance:

Peter passes to Riad who reverses direction and sends the ball back toward me. I settle it, step back and kick with all my strength straight ahead. The ball drops just beyond the centre spot. Sam jumps in unison with a Bluffers midfielder to head it. It strikes Sam's shoulder and rolls to the ground. Ade runs after it. He dribbles it centre toward the Bluffers penalty box area. He looks like he is checking to see that he is not kicking it to someone who might be offside. He dribbles forward and passes it to Hassan. Hassan stops it and slides it to his right to Farid who instantly shoots it directly ahead to Sam. Hassan has moved past the defender and is straight left of Sam. Sam rolls it to Hassan, who is aware of a defender charging from his left. He has no time to settle the ball. He shoots it straight ahead, just beyond the outstretched glove of the goalkeeper.

Sensational Goal! 5–1.

Less than thirty seconds were left of play.

Then, finally, the ref blew the whistle, extending his arm in the direction of the victors. The Hall United team, including assistants, celebrated on the field — hugging, high-fiving, weeping with joy — even Muhammad.

The Bluffers coach approached Coach Greenidge. They exchanged kisses on the cheek as she congratulated him.

Ozzie waved to Rebecca and Dad in the stands. He whispered to Victor before both teams lined up to shake hands. When Victor reached the Bluffers captain, Victor held out his armband, offering it to his defeated opponent. The Bluffers captain was surprised, but offered his in return. Ozzie exchanged shirts with the Bluffers goalkeeper. They were acts of compassion in action.

Coach Greenidge waved Ozzie and Victor over and introduced them to Coach Jeong-Hough. "She coaches league soccer indoors during the winter," said Mr. Greenidge.

"Congratulations, Ozzie and Victor. Goalkeepers and co-captains, a good combination of skills," she said, handing each her card. "Have your parents contact me soon if you want to play this winter."

"Thank you for giving our team this chance to play," Ozzie said.

An Act of Compassion

He looked at the card. He now had a new attitude toward change. He did not know what would be next in his life. But he felt that it would all be okay. And that made him feel excited.

Epilogue
Final Decision

"REFUGEES TEAM UP TO DEFEAT SOCCER CHAMPS" the headline in the local newspaper screamed. The paper ran a photo of co-captains Ozzie and Victor and one of the entire team with a grinning Coach Greenidge. The article quoted Coach Greenidge as saying, "Soccer is a sport full of surprises. Hard work, determination and teamwork will sometimes make the impossible possible. I'm proud of these boys."

The next day, Coach Greenidge hosted a pizza luncheon in the gym. Principal Arsenault entered and congratulated them again.

"Keep eating. I have one brief announcement to make," she started. "Area Superintendent Dominski has agreed to support a soccer program for Grade seven/eight boys and girls separately. It will start next spring in advance of next year's soccer season."

During the applause and whistles Ozzie's only thought was how Coach Greenidge's face lit up like both the sun and the moon together. By the afternoon Coach Greenidge reported that several Grade six and seven students had signed up for soccer.

"I'm glad your dreams are coming through, Coach Greenidge. Well deserved," Ozzie said.

"You had a huge hand in that, young brother. Thanks."

After all the pizza they ate, Ozzie didn't know if Dylan and Victor could eat much when they arrived for supper at the Holder house. He shouldn't have worried. Victor, tasting West Indian roti for the first time, chose one they called *I-Tal* which had seven vegetables. There were side dishes of small round flatbreads, known as doubles, stuffed with curried chickpeas and other finger foods, along with guava and mango juices. Rebecca, Indra and Fola were there too.

By the time Mom came home it was just Ozzie's family gathered in the living room.

"Today I made a decision," she began.

Here it comes, Ozzie thought. *Well, I'm prepared for it. I think.*

"I have decided to take Scarborough Centenary's offer. We will stay in Malvern."

Ozzie ran into Mom's arms. It was good that he had trusted Mom to make the decision. It was even better that she made that one.

Then Mom, Dad and Rebecca presented Ozzie with a gold chain with a gold soccer ball pendant. It left him oddly speechless. It was then that he realized that he had not put the beaded chain back on after the friendly match.

Later, Ozzie and Rebecca sat in their room.

"I'm not worried about change anymore, Sis," said Ozzie.

"But I'm glad we're staying here," said Rebecca as she left the room to wash up before sleep.

"Me, too."

Ozzie thought about what he had said to Rebecca. Yes, Ozzie was glad to be staying in Malvern. But he had prepared for a big change and had actually been looking forward to being out of his comfort zone. He wondered what a new life in Hamilton would have been like: a different environment, huge mall to explore, school with new friends.

But staying in Malvern didn't mean that everything stayed the same. He had captained a soccer team to a win. He had helped start a soccer program at his school. He now had a new friend, Victor.

Ozzie looked at Coach Jeong-Hough's card on his dresser where it sat beside his beaded chain. A winter of league soccer would be a first for him. *Bring it on!* He would think more about that tomorrow.

Ozzie placed the beaded chain in a wooden box with things he had outgrown. He touched the golden soccer ball on its chain. He liked it. It felt right. Then he opened a drawer. He lifted out the purple scarf and inhaled its scent. After all these years it still held a trace of his mother's soap. He untied the knot and looked at the cover of the book. There was still a faded crimson stain. Blood. It was his father's blood. His father had been rereading it when he and his mother disappeared from their home. *Things Fall Apart* by Chinua Achebe. The author was from his birth father's village.

Things fall apart. They do. And yet they don't, Ozzie thought.

He opened to the first page and began reading.

Acknowledgements

A heartfelt thanks to my editor, Kat Mototsune, for her diligent advice and support through the development of this book and sub-series. I look forward to producing more titles. Thanks, Jim and Team Lorimer, for continuing to publish much needed books for our youth. Super special thanks to Renee for enduring love.

I extend deep gratitude to deceased family members for instilling the love of reading and support: Mary Adelaide Barde (Nursey), Laura Barde (Aunty Laura), Yvonne Domingue (Aunty Yvonne), Joan Frederick-Jones (Aunt Joan) and Laura St. Clair Charles.

⚽ ⚽ ⚽

The author makes a special thanks to the Ontario Arts Council's Writers' Reserve Program for research and development of the manuscript.